THE TOUCH OF MURDER

THE TALE OF THE MAGISTRATE PT. 1

JF LEE

Captain Chen Yong

Captain Chen is the leader of Magistrate Tao Jun's staff. A sharp young man with a dry sense of humor, he takes his duties very seriously and is dependable.

Officer Ruo Bao

Officer Ruo is the muscle. A large and imposing man, his simple expressions hide a keen investigative mind.

OTHER CHARACTERS

Bai Jingyi

A young merchant woman that runs the Righteous Will escort company. A formidable practitioner of her family's Flying Spear technique. She hires fighters from the *jianghu* to help out with the business.

Yan Tao

The friendly proprietor of the Green Brocade Inn (also known as the Broken Furniture Inn). The inn is popular place in the *jianghu* and attracts visitors from all walks of life. The inn got its reputation from the sheer number of fights that always broke out in the place. His fortunes changed when a mysterious young girl came to his restaurant and saved his life. Since hiring the girl, he has renovated the inn with an arena to accommodate fighters. Yan Tao's business is booming.

Miao

A serving girl and bouncer at the Green Brocade Inn, Miao is a girl with a mysterious past. Showing up one day at the inn with no recollection of who she was, she showed remarkable martial skill in defending Yan Tao and the inn from a gang of thugs. In gratitude, Yan Tao gave her a home, a job, and all the *bao* she could eat.

————

1

THE LACQUER ON THE CEILING BEAMS ABOVE MY DESK WAS peeling—I was sure of it. Worse still, the red paint was chipping. I could see thin flecks of it threatening to drift down onto the floor below. I wondered when the last time anyone repainted up there.

I am bored.

When you spend your day thinking about paint chips, that's when you know you're bored. But bored was good. I don't get enough bored days. And besides, you have to be vigilant about paint chips and stuff like that. I mean these are important things. For one, I can't be a good magistrate knowing that I've got paint flecks on my robes. What an embarrassment.

I wore a brand new robe to work today, one with that deep rich blue and threaded with silk. And if there's anything I've learned in life, it's that if you're wearing a new robe, then a mess is waiting for you. The last time I wore a new robe to the tribunal, a crazy man with a knife came in and held one of the clerks hostage. Everyone was running around in a panic, and it was definitely more exciting than the paperwork, but it ended up with blood splatters on my new robe, and it was stained beyond repair. [1]

Maybe I should move to a different desk. Maybe move my desk across the room?

"Magistrate Tao Jun! Are you paying attention?" my adjutant said. Ji Ping had the kind of grating voice that could waken a hermit from a decade-long meditation. It was part of why I kept him around, but heavens if it didn't hurt the ears.

Right, I'm not supposed to be bored.

"Of course, I'm paying attention to you," I chuckled trying to deflect his irritation. This was, of course, a lie. I knew he didn't believe me, but it was a habit, the game we play.

"Sure," he said dryly.

"Ji Ping, you're as bad as my wife," I chided.

"The woman must be an incarnation of the goddess of mercy to put up with you," he glared. Yep, he didn't believe me. He wins this round, I guess.

"I'm still your boss," I warned. "I can fire you."

"You won't do that," he said, and there was almost a sneer in there. "You can't find anyone else who can do what I can do."

He was right. Good help was hard to find around here. It didn't matter how far up you were in the imperial bureaucracy. If you weren't careful, the other government officials would poach your staff. Without Ji Ping, I'd be in big trouble. He did all those little things that I never wanted to do. He tried to keep me on a proper schedule and up-to-date with all those 'proper' magistrate things I hate. And he had a memory better than an angry wife with a litany of mistakes to bring down on your head like the judgement of heaven. It made organizing the details of a case easier when all I had to do was look at him and he'd spout everything under the sun.

I don't like telling him how much of a help he is. Better to leave him feeling unappreciated. Keeps him grouchy and sharp. A good man, if a little bit high strung.

Ji Ping was the kind of guy born to be a career bureaucrat and lived to be a bureaucrat. He was a short kind of guy with a round face. He typically wore a *futou*[2] to cover the signs of his baldness. He stroked a greying beard of wisps when he pondered. He didn't have any family, so he was basically married to his job. That meant he was all kinds of by the book. He loved the official's uniform and kept it in as tidy order as you could.

"Keep it simple, Ji Ping," I said yawning. "Just the basics."

He scowled, then unfolded the bulletin again. A chill breeze swept in through the open window of the office, causing everyone to momentarily reach for fluttering papers. I tried not to shiver. It wouldn't do for anyone to see their boss shiver.

"The tribunal in Tu'men has no leads on the caravan attack from three months ago. They are requesting our assistance," Adjutant Ji Ping said. His matter-of-fact tone was sure to set the rest of my staff off.

"I don't see how we can help," Captain Chen said, crossing his arms angrily. And there it was. I don't blame him for being annoyed—those slackers in Tu'men were always crying for help. *Oh no! I can't find my shoes! Better send a missive to the tribunal in An'lin for help.* Idiots.

Captain Chen was a sharp young man with a face that was all angles, though there were creases on his face that marked the permanent frown that he wore. He had a dry sense of humor that I appreciated. I liked the way he got under Ji Ping's skin, just like I liked the way Ji Ping got under his skin. I kept Captain Chen around because he was responsible—the kind of guy you want running the show when you weren't there. He had a good career ahead of him, and he was definitely going places. Well, he would go places if I ever let him out of my staff. Good help is hard to find after all.

"It's not like we know anything that they don't. Probably just bandits, right?"

Ji Ping shook his head. "Not bandits."

"Black Tiger Rebels?" Officer Ruo spoke up, a crooked smile reaching for his beady eyes playing across his face. He had a slow way of speaking and a deep voice that seemed fitting for his size. He's a big, big, big man, with long muscular arms and a torso as big as an ox. He kind of looked like an ox, too, now that I think about it, but don't let that size fool you. He's faster than he looks. He's great in a fight and intimidating. He just shows up and people respond. Probably because they like how he looks in the uniform. Or they're scared because of how he just towers over everyone. Either way, despite his cow face (because of?) it made him popular with the ladies, though he didn't realize it. Still, he had a good nose for investigative work, and he was a big body. Good reasons to keep him around.

"Not rebels either," Ji Ping said, shaking his head. "Something else."

"If it's not rebels or bandits, then what?" Captain Chen asked.

"I said, 'Something else'."

"Something else," Captain Chen mocked. "For someone that knows so much, you don't know anything, do you?"

Ji Ping and Captain Chen had a healthy dislike for each other. They were always butting heads, but they worked amazingly well together. I knew it, they knew it, everyone knew it. But just because everyone knew it didn't mean they were ever going to admit it. You'd sooner pry a pork bone from a hungry dog than get those two to say nice things about each other.

"Did we ever get the details?" Captain Chen asked.

"I already said it. If you were paying attention, then you'd get the details." It was Captain Chen's turn to be under Ji Ping's baleful glare. "It was a precision strike with archers to take out the main guards. The officials guarding the gold ingots had their throats cut. Tidy cuts, apparently."

"Tidy?"

"That's what Magistrate Pao said in his report. I'm just reading you what he wrote. They included a person of interest—a sketch."

"That's new," I said. "Let's see it."

Ji Ping handed over the paper with the sketch of the suspect, but not without grumbling about how no one listened to him. I didn't catch it. I wasn't listening.

"Geez, this is a good-looking guy," Captain Chen let out a whistle. "Feels like he should be the hero of a story, not the bad guy."

"Pretty people can be bad, Captain Chen. I mean, just look at my wife . . ." I said.

"The caravan was the decoy. What about the real messenger?" Captain Chen asked.

I remembered when we first discussed this plan with the treasury minister. He thought he had a stroke of genius and wore that stupid, smug expression for weeks. Since the Black Tiger rebels had started attacking convoys, the military thought they'd be smart and use decoys and backups so everything couldn't be taken at once. Things didn't quite work out for him.

"They found them dead in a ditch, just outside of Tu'men."

"Throats slit too?"

"No, this was more subtle. Poison."

"Poison?" said Officer Ruo.

"What kind of poison?" asked Captain Chen.

I knew this answer. "Qiang Ge's Tears."

Ji Ping looked at me, surprised. "I didn't think you were paying attention."

"Come on, Ji Ping, give me some credit. I'm smarter than you think."

"Uh-huh."

The truth is that I'm a damn good magistrate because I

notice the details. And it's details like this type of poison that worried me. Violent attacks could be attributed to rebels or bandits. Poison, on the other hand, required a different sort of planning. I had some experience with this poison in the past, and while it wasn't an overly dramatic poison like those that made people spit up blood and die, it had its uses.

"The three men in the decoy convoy were well trained in *wugong*[3]—probably some of the best in the governor's guard. Only the poison Qiang Ge's Tears could have disrupted their qi flow enough to render them so helpless," I said. I didn't think it was possible, but Captain Chen's frown deepened. Officer Ruo looked deep in thought, or maybe he wasn't having any thoughts.

"You're right, Magistrate. The coroner's report confirmed evidence of Qiang Ge's tears," Ji Ping said, impressed. "Tu'men also wants us on the lookout for persons of interest in the fireworks incident. They think it's connected to the robbery."

"Still? The explosion at the factory was three weeks ago," Captain Chen complained. "The whole place burned, didn't it? And we're in a completely different city. How are we supposed to find clues here?"

"We have a description of the suspect at least," Ji Ping said, pointing to the sketch. "They think it's the same guy."

"A description? I thought they said that everyone involved died in the fire. What are those idiots in Tu'men doing?" Captain Chen cursed. "Are they really that incompetent?"

"They're not incompetent," Ji Ping snapped.

"Oh, you're going to defend them?" Captain Chen bit back. "You were complaining about them yesterday."

"They're only about as incompetent as you."

I left them to their bickering and slouched in the stiff wooden chair.

Hearing the details of the attack again made me groan

inwardly. This case of the missing treasury messenger was bad news, and since the Treasury Minister couldn't find his belt if it was tied to his waist, I knew that I was going to get dragged into it.

And everything had been going so well today.

The day started off with a good breakfast. The new cook the wife hired was a real talent. Maybe even a divine talent. He somehow makes the simple things like rice congee and fried *youtiao*[4] seem absolutely decadent. It was delicious enough for me to slip away into that wonderful space that I can ignore the nagging and yelling my wife likes to heap upon me.

I usually don't respond to her jibes. Then she says that I'm distant and that I should spend more time with the family. Well, I would if I wasn't going to get yelled at all the time, right?

But that's nothing new.

Captain Chen frowned at me. "We're wasting our time. We should be looking for the Black Tiger rebels."

"And how are you going to look for them? Just charge off into the woods and hope for the best?" Ji Ping retorted.

I tuned out their arguing again. Lunch couldn't come soon enough. Something delicious? Maybe braised beef, steamed *jielan*[5], and a bowl of rice. I could slip home and get something to eat, maybe even avoid the angry wife. But I'd have to be discreet, stealthy even. I couldn't let any of the servants know—they were on her side. I shook my head. How did it come to this? Going home for lunch required as much planning as a heist.

A chill breeze came through the open window again, sweeping up the papers on our desks. Ji Ping and Captain Chen cursed and hurried to gather the scattered paper. They yelled at Ruo to help, but with his big frame, he only made things worse by knocking over more paper. Another gust of wind came through, and the papers scattered some more. I suppose I could have helped them, but it was fun to watch them scurry around the room chasing paper.

At least that put an end to the arguing.

The office we occupied was the large chamber in the east wing of An'lin's tribunal building. Spacious and cold, and far bigger than I needed. Despite it being the 'best' office in the building with beautiful scrollwork on the room's pillars, I didn't like spending time here. Too pretentious—a byproduct of the governor's constant desire to promote me, even when I don't want it[6].

Especially when I don't want it.

I guess that's the pain of being good at what you do.

If there's something you should know about me, it's that I'm not quite a normal magistrate. A normal magistrate is a function of the imperial bureaucracy. They're on the lower rungs of the governmental ladder. They are overworked people that have to deal with tax collection, passing laws, registering births, updating the land registry . . . all the boring stuff that keeps the kingdom running. They scurry around with clerks and piles of documents that all seem very important.

Sometimes, if you're lucky, you get tasked with investigating special cases. Sometimes if you're really lucky, you do well at your job and someone somewhere recognizes your talents and says something about it to the right somebody, and before you know it, you end up in a capital city like An'lin. Apparently, the governor liked the way I 'burned'[7] away his bandit problem in the town of Gan'long.

When I returned to An'lin, the governor greeted me with a big smile, then handed me a shiny new seal and wanted to make me a prefect, answerable only to him. I didn't like the idea of all that responsibility and paperwork, so I told him I was going to retire. He then came back to me with an even bigger grin and pushed the seal into my hands, basically ignoring me. He then announced to his staff that Magistrate

Tao Jun had broad authority to act as his 'special investigator to the judicature and tribunal'—a fancy title later ratified by the emperor. He then booted Wang Yao out of his office, gave those chambers to me, and then went on his way. I think he feels like he accomplished something big, getting me to stay in his province.

Well, all things considered, a big city appointment. A good sign in my career, or as my father would put it, "Finally making something of my useless life."

So there I was, making something of my useless life by studying the central beams of the ceiling, leaned back in my chair. I eyed the paint suspiciously. I'd have to get someone to touch up the place. To be honest, I'd rather spend my time worrying about mundane things than the stuff my staff were arguing about. Oh, I'm sure I could have spent some time thinking about the missing treasury money, but those were problems for tomorrow. Why worry about something you can't control?

I tipped my *futou* back so I wouldn't have to see the disapproving glare of my adjutant, Ji Ping. The man never knew how to relax. It was dark inside my hat, and smelled kind of musty too. I thought about getting a quick nap if not lunch. I sometimes get a nap in when Ji Ping wasn't around. The other officers don't mind when I nap—I'm their boss, after all. But Ji Ping? He says he's doing me a favor by tipping my chair and jerking me awake.

"It's not proper for a magistrate to be napping on the job!" he would shriek. I'm not exaggerating; shriek is the right word, and the man's voice could carry. It's a good thing this office was so large, or else I'm sure the other officials in the building would come wondering what was going on.

I couldn't fault him, though. I'm probably[8] difficult to work with.

I was enjoying the dark shade of my hat when I heard him cough—the kind that was supposed to get your attention in a discreet but not so discreet way. I decided to ignore it. Then came another cough. And then another.

This is the part of the story where my day turned from average to bad really fast. You know that feeling you get when you just *know* that you're going to catch it? Like that moment when you get home and you've barely stepped inside the doorway and your wife fixes you with a glare that could shave all the hair off your head and leave you balder than a monk receiving his ordination scars?

That feeling.

"Hello, *Magistrate* Tao Jun," a voice said. Female. There was something about the way she said magistrate, that clearly showed how much she really thought about my position.

I lifted my hat a crack and took a peek.

Bai Jingyi.

She stood smirking, with her arms folded across her chest. She had part of her hair up in a bun, the rest cascading over her shoulders behind her. A fur-lined vest rested over her merchant clothes, and she wore dark blue pants with boots that were caked with a bit of mud. She was tall and powerfully built and moved with the confidence of a warrior.

Or two warriors.

I'd seen her in action, and she could easily hold her own against more than her fair share. She didn't have her spear with her, but that didn't make her any less dangerous. An equally cunning warrior and businesswoman, Bai Jingyi inherited the Righteous Will company after her father retired. Old man Bai was a smart businessman, and his daughter was even smarter. She was also a master of her family's Flying Spear technique, which meant she knew how to protect her family's business assets with the point of her weapon.

A very emphatic point.

I should have just said no without hearing her out and sent her hurrying back out the door. But I'll admit, I was curious. And I wasn't one to say no to a pretty face. Even if her pretty face came with a fist that could knock a man out cold without messing up her hair.

It's always a woman—pretty one, ugly one, it's all the same. Look, I have nothing against women. But their problems almost always try to get me killed.

"To what do I owe the pleasure, Bai *xiaojie*⁹*?*" I said dryly with a smile.

"I'm missing someone."

"So, you need something to mend a broken heart? I know a couple of inns that serve a good wine that can help. Or you might want a matchmaker."

She arced an eyebrow at my comment, and I smirked. It was fun to ruffle her feathers.

"One of my people is missing," she corrected. "I need your help to find him. Huang Lian."

"You're well connected in the *jianghu*¹⁰," I said. "Why come here?"

"It has to be aboveboard. I need official help."

"I see . . ."

She leaned out with her head, doing some kind of strange nodding thing.

"What are you doing? Why do you keep doing this?" I made the head gesture she was doing.

She let out an exasperated breath. "I'm trying to tell you to dismiss your people."

"Oh," I said. "Right."

I gestured at adjutant Ji Ping and Captain Chen. Ji Ping sputtered a protest, but Officer Ruo grabbed him, hauled him to his feet, and hustled him out the door. Captain Chen was already out the door.

"Come on, let's get some tea," Officer Ruo said.

I smiled. I needed to give him a raise.

When they had left, I gestured for her to sit. She shook her head, opting to pace around the room instead.

"Why don't you start from the beginning?" I asked, but as

she took a deep breath to start, I shook my head. "Actually, why don't you start from the middle? Save me some time."

"The censorate," she middled, annoyed. "They're investigating me."

"I see," I said, nodding grimly. The censorate were bad news. Imagine a perfectly sunny summer day and then having it turn into a frigid snowstorm. That's what it's like dealing with the censorate. The emperor's personal investigation unit had the ability to turn a good day into a horrible, terrible, absolutely rotten day, just by showing up. So rotten. Rotten eggs and maggot-filled meat rotten. "Did you do something wrong?"

"Of course not!" She said quickly. Maybe a little too quickly. We all had things to hide from the censorate. Even I did.

"Then why are you under investigation?"

She sped through the story. Something about smugglers having infiltrated her organization and using her company to smuggle weapons to the Black Tiger rebels. I nodded grimly. That was the sort of thing that invited Imperial attention and not the local authority either. I was following some leads on the Black Tigers myself, but Censorate attention would execute your clan to the eighth degree. It turned out that they had sent their own spy to infiltrate Righteous Will, and they turned up dead as well, the culprit in the wind[11].

No wonder she was being careful.

"So they're looking at all your jianghu connections—both legal and less legal."

"We all need those connections to do business. You know that."

I nodded.

"But they're not so understanding."

"It's all that time spent in the capital. They don't understand how things are done out here in the real world," I shrugged. I remembered the times I visited my father in the capital. It really did feel like a different life there.

"Are you going to help me?"

"Bai xiaojie, I don't even know what I'm supposed to be doing yet."

"Find Huang Lian. Something is wrong here."

"What's in it for me?"

"The satisfaction of doing your job?"

I frowned at her.

"How about the chance to get out of your office?"

"What's wrong with my office?"

"Nothing. But I can tell you don't like being here."

"What gave you that idea?"

"The fact that you stayed out on the road with Li Ming and I for a couple of months," she said, referring to our time at the Eastern Cedar Temple[12].

She wasn't entirely wrong. It wasn't that long ago that I was trying to help my sworn brother, Li Ming, find his daughter/not daughter. Sometime in the last year he had taken up a stray—a runaway serving girl from the pleasure houses of Tu'men[13]. On the way out, she managed to maim a nobleman's son, and somehow managed to convince my irascible brother to take her in to his custody. Despite his protests, I was sure that he saw her as a daughter, one to replace the little girl he lost years ago. He claimed that she wasn't his apprentice either, and that's the kind of self-deception that makes me roll my eyes. I liked her well enough. She had spunk, and a good kick. My shins can attest to that.

Sadly, imperial justice is far from perfect and sometimes harms the people you want to protect. The bounty hunters found her. Li Ming roped me and Jingyi into searching for her, and it still burns me that we were too late. Wherever she went, it was far enough away that the trail went cold.

I spared a thought for my brother—wherever he was.

"I was injured." And feverish. And hurting in a hundred places. I haven't been that beat up in a while. I didn't like it.

She shrugged. "You still could have come back to the city."

"I did come back."

"Not before you had to," she said. "I seem to recall an eloquent speech about doing what was right for the people?"

"Fine, tell me about this guy," I said, not wanting to argue about it.

I listened to her drone on about the guy, something about how he was the Righteous Will's lead finder and how he'd worked for the family for decades. He'd scout out possible clients and valuable goods to transport. He had a few hangouts in An'lin, some other familiar jaunts in this part of the town. I wished I hadn't dismissed Ji Ping. He was better at taking care of the details and collecting information.

Me? I do my thing best. I put it all together. There's a sort of feel that comes from every case, and there comes a point where the threads just kind of make sense. The beginning when someone was telling their sob story was not that point.

"Hey, are you paying attention?" Jingyi asked.

"Yeah, yeah," I nodded. "Of course I am. So this has nothing to do with a broken heart."

"I thought I told you . . ."

"I mean, it sounds like the man was married to his job. No room for a broken heart."

Jingyi frowned and shook her head. "I don't think he ever had anyone special."

"What was he doing?"

She leaned in over my desk.

"He was looking into the treasury hit."

I raised an eyebrow. "You know about that?"

"Everyone knows about it. Those guys protecting your main convoy, I knew them. They were some of the best in the business. An attack like that is enough to set us all on edge."

It sounded like a good answer, and I should have accepted it. Maybe I was in a bad mood, but I didn't. "I don't buy it. Try again."

She glared at me, and I met her gaze with an impassive shrug. Finally, she gave in.

"I sent him to do some digging around because I thought that if we could figure out what happened, we could get some of this heat from the censorate off our backs," she said with a deep long sigh, the kind that feels world weary.

"Okay, so I need to go find this guy—"

"Huang Lian."

"—Huang Lian. What's in it for me?"

"Other than doing your job?" she seemed taken aback by the question.

"Bai xiaojie, you have been around the jianghu long enough to not be *that* naive. I have so many other things that I could be doing," I said, pointing at the pile of paperwork on my desk. "Why should I put your missing person on the top of my workload?"

"I'll owe you a favor?" Jingyi grimaced. It was the same look most people gave me at the prospect of owing me. I gave her my most charming grin. Some people collect weapons. Some people collect wealth or power. But me? I collect favors. You really can't have too many favors owed.

And I always collect.

2
___

A MISSING PERSON, EH? NOT TO BRAG OR ANYTHING, BUT I AM actually pretty good at finding missing people. Over the years, I've picked up a few skills that help me find people, put a happy end to good cases.

But like I said, this was not a good case.

I called my staff in for a quick briefing. As I expected, Ji Ping gave me a skeptical look about the legitimacy of the case. He wasn't much for working with people deeply rooted in the *jianghu*, but he didn't raise any concerns other than his disdain, which I could handle. Captain Chen and Officer Ruo nodded as I laid out their assignments and the neighborhoods they would canvas. They would do the obvious stuff—hitting up friends and local haunts for information about him. You'd be surprised how often the obvious stuff turns up the right answers.

Other magistrates would let their people go and do the work and wait for them to come back. Not me. I prefer to get a feel for things myself. I grabbed my sword as I left the office. It's a brilliant white sword—Joy—a relic of the Chang'sha monastery, and one of the treasures of Blue Mountain. It's a piece from a different age, a different life. I never go anywhere without it. Sure, lugging a sword everywhere is a bit of a burden and makes things complicated at worst, but it's also the swiftest friend I have. We've been through a lot together.

I headed to the shipping district, walking fast to keep the chill away. It was early in the spring, that uncomfortable time of year where the weather decided if it wants to move on from the previous season. I asked around at the customs office first for Huang Lian and heard the same story from the clerk that Jingyi told me. Not that I doubted her—she was a fairly honest type—but I wanted to make sure she was on the level. Experience taught me that you can never be too sure.

The customs office had no leads, so I headed to another contact in the area, passing along the edge of the Kuan river. The cormorants chattered over the bustle of the port. It was midmorning, and fishermen were already returning with their catches. I didn't care too much for the smell of the fish, delicious as they were, but you have to do what you have to do.

Lai Wu sat behind a cart covered with canvas near where the fishermen unloaded their catch. It was his office of sorts, though I wasn't really sure what he bought or sold there. I didn't want to know, because if I did, then I might have to actually do something about it. And if I did something about it, then everyone would be miserable, and that was not fun for me.

And the paperwork. Ugh.

As I approached, he straightened, pulling his finger out of his nose and wiping it on his shirt. Lai Wu was a short man with rapidly thinning hair that looked like greasy rat tails hanging from his scalp. He had a crooked kind of smile with yellowing and rotting teeth that gave him trouble. He definitely looked the part—a shady guy that somehow had his fingers in everything. I investigated him once, and to my utter astonishment found that he was clean. Mostly, anyway.

As it was, he had the right connections to the right people and knew what was going on in town. I was pretty sure he had ties to the Beggar Sect, the mysterious organization of vagabonds and mendicants that spanned the length of the empire and beyond.

"Magistrate! Just the person I was looking for. Listen, I need your help
. . ." he started.

"You always need my help," I said, cutting him off.

"It's not my fault."

"It's also never your fault," I said wearily. I started lifting the edge of the canvas covering his cart. "Do you really want me to poke around and find out if I'm right? It won't be pretty."

"Fine, fine. What do you want?" He groused, smoothing out the canvas. I let go.

"Huang Lian, guy that works with Righteous Will."

"Oh yeah, I know him. Good guy. What's up? Something wrong with him?" Lai Wu asked.

"Gone missing, apparently."

"That's not good."

"You have anything else to add?"

"Now that you mention it, I haven't seen him in a while."

"That's . . . not helpful. You know what, I think I need to do a little poking around here," I said, lifting up the canvas again covering his cart. I caught the sheen of some fine pottery. Obviously not his.

"Okay, last I heard, he was looking to move some different kind of cargo," he said, pushing a hand down on the canvas again and glaring at me.

"What kind of cargo?" I asked, my eyes narrowing.

"Nothing too crazy. I think it was more of a someone than a something."

"Slave? Bai Jingyi would never allow that," I said.

"Oh, nothing like that," he quickly added. "Just someone that didn't want to be noticed."

"Interesting . . . You sure know a lot about this."

He shrugged. "I just hear things."

"Did you hear where to find him?"

"He's not in the city—that much I do know," he shrugged again.

I was about to turn and leave when he spoke up again. "Hey, uh. Did you guys figure out that treasury caravan raid?"

"You know something about it?"

"No, no, no. Well, maybe."

"Cough it up."

"Word in the *jianghu* is that the Hidden Fist were involved."

I almost laughed out loud. "An assassin sect was involved with a caravan hit?"

"Hey, stranger things have happened. What with the Black Tiger rebellion going on? Maybe they needed the extra muscle."

"Sure, sure," I laughed. Hidden Fist indeed. "Thanks for your help, Lai Wu, and get rid of that vase before the next patrol comes by or else there'll be hell to pay."

"Oh, come on! I just helped you!"

"And I'm helping you!" I called back.

Lunch time.

My feet were tired from walking around all morning. I was hungry and ready to sit down for a bit. To tell the truth, I've been hungry since breakfast.

I also needed a drink.

I walked to the Golden Ingot restaurant where I knew my officers were hanging out. We had a routine down—a few hours canvassing the neighborhoods and then a report. They were sitting on the second floor at their usual table in the corner. Daylight spilled in through the open window beside them. Captain Chen and Officer Ruo raised a cup in greeting, and Ji Ping glowered at me and then at them. The glower was for show. He had his own small jar of wine at his side.

The Golden Ingot was one of the favorites of government officials. It was close to the administration buildings and free of the usual riff-raff that might enter. The proprietor had a reputation of discretion and was paid handsomely for it. I had some suspicion that he was connected to someone's information network, but I didn't want to know.

I set Joy down by the table as I settled down next to them and took a quick peek out the window. I shivered as another chill breeze blew through the window. Below us the busy streets of An'lin and the commerce of the city flowed in their never ending patterns. Carts trundling down cobblestone roads. Coolies carrying canvas wrapped supplies. The call of barkers and merchants drifting on the breeze.

"Anything good?" I asked them.

"A *popo* beat her grandson when he wouldn't hold her hand," Officer Ruo reported, turning his attention back to the window. "Quiet day otherwise."

"I meant with our missing person—Huang Lian," I corrected, annoyed.

"Oh, then I've got nothing," Officer Ruo said. "A lot of merchants are worried after that caravan attack."

"How does everyone know about that?" I shook my head. For all the efforts the treasury made to keep things quiet, that story sure spread.

"What are we doing, boss? Does this Huang Lian have something to do with the attack?"

"Yeah, what's this about anyway?" Captain Chen asked, pouring me a drink. The wine gave me some much needed warmth. I need to give this man a raise. I told them in short what was going on, reviewing the details we knew. A missing person, one unusually married to his job. Usually talking it over with my people helps me figure out where to go with the case. Especially with a missing person. It takes a while to figure out where they might have gone.

"You said Bai Jingyi gave you this case?" Ji Ping asked, without turning towards us. He would never admit it, but he always liked looking out the window.

"Wait, wait, wait, wait, wait," Officer Ruo said, holding his hands up. A wild and excited look in his eyes. "Bai Jingyi? *THE* Bai Jingyi?"

"You know her?"

"Know her? She's a celebrity. She has a huge following!" Officer Ruo said.

"Wow, we get to work for Bai Jingyi on this case," Captain Chen said, his eyes widening. "Wait, that means that woman that was in the office . . ."

". . . was Bai Jingyi!" Officer Ruo groaned. "I would have gotten an autograph if I had known."

"You're not working for her. You're still working for me. Last I checked, I was the one that paid you a salary."

You see what I have to put up with?

Officer Ruo sat back down, but he still wore a starstruck expression on his face. "I need to have her sign something. Do you think she'd sign my sword?"

"Ink doesn't stay on the sword very long," Ji Ping said. "I tried."

"Enough about Bai Jingyi. Someone tell me something good about our missing person," I growled.

Before anyone could answer, a rotund man with a thin goatee placed a hand on our table. We looked up at him, startled that anyone would interrupt us. This was our safe place. No one bothered us at the Golden Ingot. He leaned over us, desperation in his eyes. He stank of sweat, and it streamed down his face.

"Please help me. Someone is after me."

"You can't be here!" the proprietor hurried to the man's side, tugging him away. "I'm so sorry, Magistrate."

"It's fine," I said, waving a dismissing hand. I took a sip of wine. "What's going on?"

"My name is Huang Lian," the man said, falling to his knees. He tried to grab onto my robes, but I moved out of the way. I've had bloody handprints on my robes before, and that is hard to clean.[1]

"Hey boss, I solved the missing person case. He's right here," Captain Chen said.

"Quiet, you fool," I chided, then turned my attention to the bleeding man. "What's going on? Bai Jingyi came to see me earlier today. She said you've been missing for days."

"I need help. Someone is trying to kill me."

"You said that already, but who—?"

"Look out!" Ji Ping yelled.

Without thinking, I ducked, but my action left our guest in full view of the window. The arrow took him in the heart. I knew he was dead before he hit the ground. *I must be getting old.* I thought. I should have seen the archer long before the arrow flew. As it was, Ji Ping's warning was a fraction late, and the second arrow tore a rip in my sleeve. My favorite robe too. Damn.

The third arrow I knocked away with my unsheathed sword.

"Stay with him! I'm in pursuit!" I yelled.

"Wait, magistrate!" Ji Ping called after me. "You can't go!"

But I was already gone, leaping out of the window onto the awning below. I watched as across the busy street the archer leaped from rooftop to building.

Qinggong.[2] *Great.* I growled. My mastery of qinggong was limited at best. I preferred to keep fights on solid ground. I leaped across to the adjoining roof, using a combination of speed and old-fashioned muscle to climb up the roof. My body protested. My wounds had healed well, but they still ached occasionally. Today was one of those days. I was rewarded for my efforts with an arrow that pierced the tile where my hand was a moment ago. I whipped Joy around in a defensive posture.

"Stop!" I yelled. "I just want to chat."

They didn't answer, but I really didn't expect them to.

"I just want to be friends!" I called out. "Won't you be my friend?"

"Stay away!" a male voice called back.

On the building across the street, I saw the archer running across the rooftop. I vaulted over the ridge of the green tiled roof, drawing on my qinggong to clear the street, but it was already too late. The archer had too much of a head start. There was no way I could catch him.

I sighed.

If there's anything that makes a case more interesting, it's an arrow fired at your heart. I had a feeling that I would be meeting this archer again, and we were only just beginning our little friendship.

By the time I got back to my men in the Golden Ingot (jumping down to the ground floor and then climbing the stairs inside, trust me it's a lot more decent for a magistrate to take the door than the window), I was sweaty, and there was a rip in my sleeve of my favorite robe.

My men had set Huang Lian's body down on the floor, covering it with a tablecloth. The distraught proprietor tried to calm his equally distraught wife. I bent down by the body, reached out a hand to touch his wrist. Still warm—warm enough that I would have thought he was still alive. But Huang Lian was dead. I knew that was the case when I leaped out of the window. Sometimes you hope that these things work out and you get what you need—like one of those desperate, gasping conversations when they tell you everything you need to know? It happens all the time in the stories.

They often don't in real life.

My officers had already checked the man's pockets and pouch for anything useful, and they shook their heads at me as I walked in. The proprietor of the restaurant still hovered nearby. His distress had now turned to muttering and cursing under his breath. I put a reassuring hand on his shoulder, told him to send my office the bill for any damages and he seemed a little mollified.

A little. It just meant his muttering was at a lower volume than before.

I sighed. This was going to be a scandal. And there's nothing An'lin loves more than a good scandal.

Huang Lian looked peaceful—at least as peaceful as he could be with an arrow in his chest.

"Anything?" I asked.

Ji Ping coughed, pulling out the arrow. He winced, wiped the blood on the dead man's robes. "Special kind of arrowhead. Barbed. The nock is made out of deer antler."

"Barbed? They're using good quality stuff." I nodded in approval. "Not just a regular criminal hit. Assassins?"

"Most likely, Excellency," Ji Ping said.

What do you know? Lai Wu might have been on to something. I wasn't familiar with the Hidden Fist's gear, but it was a possibility.

"I don't recognize the arrows, though. Any ideas?"

"No, Excellency," Ji Ping said again. I frowned. If he didn't know, then that was saying something. The man had enough useless knowledge packed into his head to fill two academies.

"What else do we have?"

"A few coins, a bit of string. He carried a small dagger," Captain Chen said, "Oh and this."

He handed me a piece of paper. It was an advertisement:

NOW AT THE GREEN BROCADE INN:
Fights while you feast!
Watch challengers from all over the *wu'lin* battle in our newly constructed arena.
Come for the brawl, and stay for the food!
This month only—The renowned acrobatic troupe, Master Lei's Cyclone Defenders, are performing reenactments from famous stories in history.

"A newly constructed arena?" I read out, mostly to myself.

"Oh yes," Ji Ping answered. "The Green Brocade Inn has undergone some major changes in the last while. It's drawing quite the crowd these days."

"Well, what do you know? Old Yan Tao is making something of the old Broken Furniture Inn."

"*Green Brocade Inn,*" Ji Ping corrected. I hated it when he did that. "The fights are quite popular. Last week Master Flying Bear defeated the Boulder in a three round brawl."

Officer Ruo and Captain Chen gaped at him. I raised an eyebrow. "I thought you didn't care much for the *jianghu*."

"I like hearing about the fights," he said in a huff.

"I like those fights too," Officer Ruo said with a grin. "Let's go watch one sometime, Ji Ping!"

Ji Ping scowled at him.

"So, what do we have then?" I said, reviewing the facts. "We've got Bai Jingyi's missing person here, dead, likely killed by an assassin's arrow."

"He was carrying an advertisement. He must have passed by Green Brocade," Captain Chen said.

"Right, good thinking," I said. The man nodded solemnly, but I could tell it made him happy. "Anyone recognize the assassin's arrow?"

Officer Ruo and Captain Chen shook their heads.

"Well, we've got more questions than answers now. It's time to change that." I said. I nodded to my officers. "Let's go to work."

"Yes, Magistrate!" they saluted.

"Get me Bai Jingyi."

One of the nice things about being a magistrate? Issuing a summons and having people respond to it. I summoned Bai Jingyi to my office, where not a few hours ago, she was asking me to help find Huang Lian. Now she was back to account for his death.

It was evening, and most of the other officials had left for the day. There were only a few clerks that stayed in the evening—those poor saps that keep the paperwork processed and the lifeblood of the kingdom moving. Well, I guess I count for a poor sap, too, working into the evening.

A servant came in to light the remaining candles and lanterns of my office. I stood by the open window and let the woman do her work. The last light of dusk set in the sky. Outside, the lights of An'lin flickered to life as hanging paper lanterns were lit. I gripped the red lacquered lattice, squeezing it tight enough in my grip that the wood creaked faintly.

Ji Ping coughed to catch my attention. Jingyi had arrived alone, without the need of an armed escort. That was good. I'd hate to have to drag a friend in under guard. Not to say I wouldn't, but I just don't like doing it. She came alone, which was also good. It meant we could have an open and honest discussion about what was going on here. But there was something that was bothering me about this case. Something close to the surface that I couldn't quite put my finger on yet.

I dismissed my staff, and Officer Ruo lingered, looking

like he wanted to protest, but I waved him away. I'd make sure he got his autograph later.

"Huang Lian is dead," I said, without getting into the pleasantries. I still leaned against the window, not bothering to sit. A cool breeze swept in from the window, causing the candles to flicker. In the distance, the call of restaurant barkers trying to lure customers to their establishments.

"What?" she asked. There was visible shock in her face, and she stumbled back as though struck. Good signs. She was too honest a woman to be able to cover up this kind of thing. I didn't actually suspect her for his death, but there were things she was hiding, things that I needed to know.

"An archer killed him."

"Who?"

"That's why you're here."

"You don't think I'd actually kill my own employee, do you?"

"Don't lie to me, Jingyi. I'm not stupid. This turned bad waaaay too quickly, which means only one thing to me. You know something. Come clean. What do you know?"

"Excuse me?" Jingyi responded. She joined me by the window, her eyebrows knit together in worry.

"You knew he was into something dangerous, didn't you? That's why you wanted me involved—I was your fall guy in case something went wrong."

She flushed.

"Well, now you have official imperial involvement, and I promise you, it can make your life miserable if you don't help me out."

"More miserable than being investigated by the censorate?"

"Much more miserable," I lied. A censorate investigation was pretty bad. I guess I could mire her in red tape. That wasn't fun for anyone. Or arrest her for some kind of made-up charge, but I wouldn't do that.

Yet.

She sighed.

"You're right. I thought if I got you involved in this, whoever was after Huang Lian would be scared off."

"It didn't work."

"Obviously," she frowned.

"You probably got him killed then."

"He's really dead then?"

"He came barging into the Golden Ingot. Died right in front of me," I showed her the rip in my robe. "They almost got me too."

She shook her head. "I don't know what happened. How did it end up like this?"

"Tell me what you know."

"Are you going to actually listen this time?" she muttered.

"I'm always listening," I lied.

She gave me a flat look, and I shrugged. "He sent word that he found someone in need of some help. He was going to arrange passage for them on one of our caravans. As soon as he got back to An'lin, things were going to happen. I was expecting him two days ago. He's never late."

"Local trouble?"

She shook her head. "I don't know. I don't usually get too involved."

"You don't see how this can be a problem?"

"There are a million things I have to take care of when running Righteous Will. I can't know what all my employees are doing," she snapped. "Besides, I trust Huang Lian. He doesn't do anything illegal."

"Trusted, you mean. Past tense. He's dead."

She flinched. I probably shouldn't have said that. It was needlessly cruel.

"He's really dead? What am I going to do without him?" she turned pale as the realization hit home.

I sighed. I was pretty sure she didn't have anything to do

with his death. "The best thing you can do right now is to help me out. Let's make sure whoever did this to him gets what they deserve."

"Justice?"

"Justice, revenge, whatever you like," I said. I started pacing. "Look, the governor is quite upset about a murder happening at one of the nicer restaurants in An'lin. He's also upset that it's somehow connected to one of the more reputable and above board security companies of the city." I gave her a thin smile. "He holds Righteous Will in very high regard, so he wants me to look into it."

"This is going to bring a lot of heat."

"Jingyi, when the censorate got involved, you were already in the fire. If we don't clear this up, it's going to be as bad as that fireworks factory explosion in Tu'men."

She shook her head. "What do you need?"

"Tell me where we need to go. If someone killed Huang Lian, then they're definitely going to kill whoever he was trying to protect. Where was he supposed to meet this person?"

Jingyi sighed. She looked tired—beyond tired—as she weighed out her decision. In a perfect world, I would have given her time to mourn, but we don't live in a perfect world. If it was perfect, I'd spend the day staring up at clouds and relaxing by the shores of a beautiful lake. Look, I hate it when bad things happen to good people. She didn't deserve this. She didn't deserve any of this, but she was involved, and I was going to get her help.

"Green Brocade Inn. Outside of An'lin. The contact didn't want to come to the city—too scared or something," she shook her head, and a sadness seemed to rest on her shoulders. "I have to take care of his funeral arrangements. But when I'm done, I'll meet you out there."

"You're going to come too? You think the censorate will let you?" I asked, surprised.

"They're going to have to," she said grimly.

After Jingyi left, I called my staff back in.

Ji Ping, Captain Chen, and Officer Ruo filed in and stood at attention.

"Pack your things. We're leaving as soon as possible."

"Where are we going?" Ji Ping complained. He didn't like being on the road. I've tried to get him to stay behind before, but he always mumbles something about someone needing to keep me out of trouble.

"We've got a fight to watch," I said, grinning at Ji Ping.

3

I'M NOT LIKE YOUR AVERAGE MAGISTRATE. SURE, I CAN SIT IN THE big chair and pronounce judgements like the rest of them. But I don't like it. Makes me feel soft. Soft like the fat rolls of the governor. Goes against my roots. Life is about being tough, not soft.

You might ask, what does a cushy magistrate, who comes from a noble family, know about tough? And you'd be right to assume otherwise. The rest of my family is soft. But me? I know a thing or two. See, when I was young, I ran away from home. I ran all the way to Blue Mountain, where I begged to become a swordsman of Blue Mountain. My head was filled with stories that our *baomu*¹ used to tell us. My siblings enjoyed the stories, too, but I was determined that I was going to be a swordsman.

It took me a month on the road to get there. And for a noble-born kid like me who didn't know anything about the wider world or the jianghu? Looking back now, I was just lucky to make it. And when I reached Blue Mountain, I thought I'd get a big hero's welcome, like they were waiting for me. Roll out the big banner and give me a big smile and welcome me into their ranks. Instead, I got a backhand to the face by old man Ye, Master Guo's personal servant. And then another backhand from Master Guo.

"You think you can just show up and expect me to teach you?"

"Uhm, yes?"

And he slapped me again. I suppose it wasn't the best of first impressions.

Master Guo wasn't particularly kind. Neither were the other students at first. But they toughened me up. Things seemed nice in that life for a while, and then Master Guo passed—murdered by the now disgraced General Shazha Kui.

We all had to grow up really fast after that. Li Ming, the master's first disciple, had it in his head to avenge Master Guo's death. I followed him on his crusade because that's just what you do. The demands of honor and all that. You grow up really quickly on the path of revenge, but it's not a good life. After a few years, that trail went cold, and with nowhere else to go, I went home.

I don't know why I expected a joyous homecoming, but I did, and I was sorely disappointed. My siblings shunned me. My father slapped me (guess you're never too old to get slapped) and my mother wouldn't speak to me for two months. But they thawed, and eventually, my father pulled some strings and got me set up in the life he thought I should be living. I was too tired to protest. Fast forward another few years, and I got tied down with an arranged marriage that neither of us really want a part of. Then I'm on the tribunal circuit, bringing justice to the enemies of the Emperor, protecting his peace and all that.

You've got to be a little tough to be a good magistrate. And I think of myself as a good magistrate. Here's the thing about this kind of work. Some of these new magistrates, they come in and think they know everything, and then they can pronounce a judgement relying on the information of their adjutants or officers. But a real magistrate, a real *good* magistrate, you've got to see what it's like yourself. Maybe you have to suffer a bit yourself. I know how the others say that it's unseemly for a magistrate to be seen investigating dingy places. But that's the only way I know how to do my job.

Plus, it's a great excuse to get out of the magistrate's office.

I get it, you know? The call of the road, the life in the jianghu. No rules, no ties beyond that of honor. I get why it's so attractive. All of these people that live in comfortable cities like An'lin or Tu'men don't get it. But I do. There's so much out there to see and do. You can be anything you want to be out there—it doesn't matter if you're male or female, noble or common. If you have the strength to prove your skill, you have a place out there.

Can you tell that I miss it?

We left early the next morning for the Green Brocade Inn. Ji Ping and Officer Ruo accompanied me. I left Captain Chen in charge of the office before we left. He didn't seem too happy about being left behind. I would have left Ji Ping, but that old nag insists on going everywhere with me now, because of how long I was absent the last time around, so he drags himself along, despite his complaints.

And Officer Ruo? Well, he's a good man, but I wouldn't leave him in charge of a brewing kettle. In fact, the last time I asked him to make tea, he practically ruined the whole package. That's a special sort of talent, I'm sure of it. But he's good for deterring would-be robbers. It's not that I can't handle a skirmish or two, but I'd rather not spill blood if I could. Too messy and I'd rather not have to explain to my wife why I got blood on yet another set of clothes.

We dressed in plain travel clothes—no official uniforms. We didn't want to scare anyone into hiding. Ji Ping said my outfit was too flashy, but what did he know? The man was married to the uniform. Me? I enjoy the fine things in life.

It was an uneventful journey. The nice chill of early spring felt good on my face, and the air smelled fresh and clean. This was why I liked to get out of An'lin and the major cities as much as possible. You kind of forget how nice it can be out there when you're stuck in an office or dealing with people's problems all day. There's a world out there, one that exists beyond the troubles of daily life. You could lose yourself staring up at the misty karst mountains all day or pondering the slow flight of a heron.

Green Brocade was only about a day's journey away from An'lin—close enough for good business, far away enough that it stays off our radar for the most part. It's technically part of a small little town named Yuan'men—the Distant Gate —that's prosperous enough but still reaps the benefits of living in the shadow of the city. Green Brocade hides a big secret. Its nickname is the Broken Furniture Inn. It has a reputation for being a bit of a rough and tumble place— where bandits and *xiake*[2] alike mingle. Sometimes they mingle too well, if you know what I mean, and it spills out into the restaurant and they break things. Thus, the nickname. Yan Tao kept a pile of broken furniture in the corner of the place. He always seemed to be adding to it. It couldn't have been good for his morale—the man always looked depressed.

But now, apparently, it was good for business.

It was mid-evening by the time we arrived, and the place was crowded. It had been a few months since I was last here, but I almost didn't recognize the place. Yan Tao had built an entire new wing to the inn, a two-story building that connected to the main restaurant. Bamboo scaffolding adorned the outside where the work crews hadn't finished. But a green tiled roof topped the addition, and it seemed like only the exterior needed finishing.

Out front, two large banners with the character for wine hung from the eaves. Red, blue, and green lanterns gave the place a warm, almost festive feel. Loud cheering came from inside the inn, accompanied by the banging of a drum and crashing of cymbals. Officer Ruo grinned a big childlike grin at me.

Ji Ping led the way to the main entrance, and Officer Ruo and I followed behind. Yan Tao was out front greeting customers with a giant grin on his face. He was a middle-aged man that was balding and tried to hide it underneath a cloth cap. The middle aged weight was beginning to weigh down his gut. For as long as I've ever known him, he was a dour man—always on the edge of anxiety or depression. To see him now, with a giant smile on his face, greeting customers like a proud father on a wedding day, was a little disconcerting. He never smiled when I dealt with him[3].

"Welcome! Welcome! Welcome to the Green Brocade Inn, I'm your host, Yan Tao and this is . . ." Sure enough, Yan Tao's smile dropped when he finally recognized me. "Oh, it's you."

"Fine greeting, Yan Tao."

"What are you doing here?" He hissed, pulling me aside away from the other customers entering the restaurant. Officer Ruo made a move to stop him, but I waved him off. Yan Tao eyed the big man nervously, taking in his size. "Are you here to cause trouble?"

"Come now, is that any greeting for an old friend?"

"Old friend?" Yan Tao growled. "You're no friend. You come here and bully me any chance you get."

"Not every chance! And I'm a generous customer," I said, wounded.

"Uh-huh," he gave me a skeptical look, then eyed my companions. I could see that he was trying to decide if we were going to cause him problems, so I knew I had to placate him.

"Look, we're just going to hang out at your inn for a bit. Have something to eat. Maybe ask a few questions. We even came in disguise to not draw any attention."

He looked me up and down. "Your disguise is terrible."

"I told you so," Ji Ping muttered. "Too flashy! But does anyone listen to me? No."

Geez. I thought I looked good. "What do you mean terrible? This is fine silk!"

"That's exactly the problem. It's too flashy for a place like this. See? Everyone's looking at you."

"Everyone's looking at me," I growled. "Because you're standing here making a big deal out of what I'm wearing." I couldn't help it. I like fine clothing. Is it my fault that everyone else is uncivilized? The feeling of that silk against my skin? Yes, please. The coarse stuff is for the peasants and monks.

"Fine, fine," Yan Tao said. He made a small wave with his hand, and a young woman with her arm in a sling appeared at his side. I didn't recognize her. Daughter? Mistress? New wife? New help? She had a pretty face in a homegrown sort of way. Pretty enough to attract attention, but not so pretty as to stop all activity on a busy market day. Those were rare. My wife was something like that, once upon a time. Before that scowl of hers took residence there.

"This is Miao, she'll take care of you. Miao, please seat these good sirs at the table in the corner."

"Yes, *laoban*," she said and then extended a hand for us to follow her. She led the way through the busy restaurant, but there was something in the way her eyes flicked over our group that caught my attention. I'd seen that look before. It was the way a fighter analyzed an opponent. She was determining if we were a threat. Then I noticed our surroundings. The customers we passed as we worked our way through the restaurant weren't watching us as we walked through the restaurant floor. They were watching *her*.

Interesting.

She wasn't very old, probably just out of her teens. But she moved with a certain confidence I've come to recognize as people with real skill. Because, you see, there's a difference.

There's a swaggering walk that comes from a petty bandit or even a low-ranking official out to bully someone. Those people are a nuisance more than anything else. But if you're just an ordinary person without any kind of training or *wugong*[4], then they'll be a problem. But with that kind of swagger, they have no real skill. You show your teeth, flex a little bit and you'll probably scare them off.

But the ones that walk with real confidence? They're the ones you have to watch out for. You show your teeth to them, you're likely to get your teeth handed back to you in handfuls. And then you might get someone else's teeth added in for good measure. That's the difference between confidence and cockiness. Sure, they both swagger, but the reasons are completely different.

I'd have to ask Ji Ping about it later. There were rumors about a *gaoshou*[5], a master that had taken up residence in the Broken Furniture Inn. Could this girl be the one?

"You're new here, aren't you?" I asked the young woman.

"Not so new. We've had a busy few months, so you might not have seen me."

"I thought I knew everyone in this place."

"Guess you don't know everyone," She smiled at me. It was a warm smile, one without any guile. You don't often meet people like that, so when you do, you better pay attention.

"Well then, I'm pleased to make your acquaintance, Miao. You can call me Jin Min," I replied, giving the first name that came to my head.

"Jin Min? Like the famous singer?" She gave me a mildly skeptical look at the name. "Where's the rest of your musical group?[6]"

"Something like that," I said. I knew that name sounded too familiar. Whatever, it was an alias, and it didn't matter if she knew it either.

"It's a pleasure, Mister Jin Min," she said. I couldn't detect any notes of mockery. She seemed sincere, and a lot nicer than that brat that my brother adopted. Miao sat us down at a table on the second floor. Up here, the clientele seemed a little better—finer looking clothes, and there was definitely a better smell. In fact, the whole area smelled new—a faint hint of the wood mixed with paint and lacquer as an undertone to plates of steaming *bao*, fish, and pork.

The place was busy. At the round tables sat travelers and locals—some that hailed from An'lin and some from beyond. There was a comfortable din to the restaurant that seemed to speak of good times and good company.

The food smelled really good, and we were hungry, so I ordered generously. Ji Ping and Ruo ate like they hadn't eaten in weeks. With the size of Ruo, I kind of expected it, but it never ceased to surprise me how much Ji Ping could put away. They sat at the side of the table with a good view of the arena, and in between mouthfuls of food, they'd make comments to each other about how the bouts were going below.

It wasn't a particularly big arena down below—octagonal shaped, maybe about five table lengths at its widest. It was smaller than some of the training areas we used back in Blue Mountain. But it seemed Yan Tao didn't spare any expense in building it. It was a raised stage and looked like it was built out of fine hardwood and other pretty solid materials. Judging by the way some of the fighters hit hard on the arena floor, it was sturdy.

Maybe he got a new carpenter.

Two combatants stood in the center of the arena—that was normal enough. Where it got strange was that each brandished a wooden stool. They swung the stools around, finding a way to incorporate them into their form.

"*Kaishi!*" a match judge shouted.

My eyes went wide as they both swung the chairs at each other like swords. The crack of their impact could be heard over the cheering crowd. Even Ji Ping and Ruo got into it. They cheered between mouthfuls of rice.

I shook my head. This was certainly new. It didn't take long before one of the combatants found an opening, and the stool swept up, catching his opponent on the chin. The man fell out of the arena, and the crowd roared again.

I was a little disappointed—neither of the stools had broken. Still, there were broken bits of furniture everywhere, and it was a wonder that anyone that fought in there didn't end up with slivers stuck in their hands and feet.

Miao passed by on her rounds, and I flagged her down. "Tell me a story."

"You'll want old man Chen Yang for that. I can get him for you."

"Not that kind of story." I shook my head. "What's with the new stage?"

"Oh that. I guess I can answer that question. Since people brawl here all the time, Yan Tao thought it would be a good idea to have a dedicated place for them to fight."

"He seems to be doing really well lately. This place was a bit of a dive before."

"It was not! It was quite charming!"

"And how do you fit into all of this?"

She smiled. It was a warm smile, but guarded. "I just happened to be passing through. I needed a place to go, and *laoban* took me in. I've been here since[7]."

"What a nice guy," I chuckled.

"He really is."

Miao cleared some of our empty dishes, and Officer Ruo gave me such a forlorn look that I rolled my eyes and ordered another plate of the *bao* that the place was famous for. He clapped happily to himself and nodded his thanks. Sometimes, it's the simple things in life.

There was something more to Miao's story and something about her that didn't make sense. The arena and Yan Tao and his crazy schemes—those fit. A merchant willing to take advantage of a situation and expand his business made sense to me. But Miao didn't.

It was something worth investigating.

The echo of a gong drew my attention back to the ring.

A man wearing a blue cape took the stage. It had gold floral print—the discards of fashion from a few years back, if I recalled correctly. Still, the crowd didn't care if he was out of date with his fashion. They cheered his arrival, and he raised his hands in a grandiose flourish. His cape and his long sleeves billowed around as he twirled.

"Oh, oh, oh!" Officer Ruo all but squealed. "It's Master Lei and the Cyclone Defenders. They're going to perform! What a great day."

"Does he remind you of anyone?" Ji Ping asked Officer Ruo. They both gave a meaningful look in my direction, then snickered.

"You keep this up and you're going to pay your own tab," I growled at them. They snickered again. I don't know why I put up with them.

"Hey boss, just enjoy the show!" said Officer Ruo good naturedly. "I've heard good things about this troupe."

"I didn't know you liked acrobatic troupes so much," Ji Ping said. He seemed surprised. I didn't blame him. I didn't know all that much about Officer Ruo. I had pegged him as a quiet kind of guy, content to play the gentle giant.

Officer Ruo was about to answer when the man below began speaking. "Thank you, thank you! My name is Master Lei, and I am the proud leader of the Cyclone Defenders. We have brought our show all the way from the East to the West and from the North to the South, and I have to say there is no better place than right here in the Green Brocade Inn. We feel absolutely at home." The crowd cheered. "We have a lovely show for you tonight—a taste of what's to come for the next few weeks in the village square."

I had to hand it to him. Master Lei had a gift for showmanship. Everyone hung on his words in eager anticipation. When he saw that he had everyone's attention, his eyes twinkled with a mischievous glint. "Please welcome to the stage, the legendary General Chao!"

Applause and cheering welcomed General Chao to the main stage. General Chao was a young man wearing a fake beard. Even with the beard on, he was a good-looking guy—I could tell from the way the young women at the restaurant suddenly perked up. Even Miao and the other wait staff were swept up in it. They leaned on the railing, putting down their tasks to get a view of the young man. I imagined Yan Tao being upset with this slacking off, and I smiled at the thought.

"There's something familiar about this young man's face . . ." Ji Ping said.

"Did you see him perform before?" Officer Ruo asked.

"I don't think so. It's been a while since I last saw one of these."

The young man unsheathed a sword from a golden scabbard with an extravagant move, and a performer on an *erhu*[8] started playing a lilting melody. A sword dance. The blade shivered and jumped from hand to hand as he leaped high and crouched low. Theatrical stuff, not good for real fighting. I could hear his footfalls on the stage too. No qinggong from what I could make out. The kid was good, but he wasn't the most amazing performer I had ever seen. The real good ones found a way to incorporate some basic qinggong into their performances to help them pull off truly astounding acrobatic feats. This kid? Not so much. Still, he had a stage presence and knew how to use his good looks to win over the crowd. The women in the crowd broke out in oohs and ahhhs.

As the performance went on, I wondered what Huang Lian was doing here. Meeting someone? This was a popular hangout for travelers and an easy enough place to keep a low profile. Either way, I suspected that Yan Tao would have some answers for me.

When the performance was over, the stage was cleared for more fights. We stayed seated at the table watching three more of the same kind of furniture match. We were rewarded with a stool shattering on the last one, and the crowd roared their approval.

At the end of the night's entertainment, Officer Ruo went off to find some wine before going to his room, and Ji Ping went with him. I stayed out at the table until the last of the customers had left. That was just fine with me. I don't need the extra protection, and I don't like having them around when I make 'inquiries.'

What they don't tell you about this job is how much talking there is. Sometimes it feels like you just go from one person to another, an endless stream of talking and talking, and you lose track of where you are after you've gone from your first contact to your fifth. You have to like talking to people to be a good magistrate. My sworn brother, Li Ming, could never do it. He hates people. He spends most of his time grumpy and glowering at people. Granted, he has a reason[9] for that, but the guy could lighten up a bit.

Maybe my wife could do all the talking. Once she gets going, she never stops. It's like being bludgeoned to death under a wall of constant chatter.

And then there's the waiting. You have to wait, and you wait until you have the right moment to talk to someone. Sure, I can come in as a full magistrate, wave my seal around and bully people into doing what I want. That works. I won't lie. But sometimes it's just easier to wait until it's convenient to have a better conversation. People are more pliable that way.

"I suppose I should thank you for waiting until everyone left before making a scene?" Yan Tao came over to my table after setting his staff cleaning. He brought over a small bottle of warm wine, poured us each a cup. He downed his in a single gulp and poured himself another cup. "So, what are you really here for? You going to bully me again? What are you up to?"

"Yan Tao, I'm hurt. Do you always think I'm up to something?" I sipped the wine. Good stuff.

"Hmph," the man snorted. "You're always up to something. You wave that magistrate token around and expect things to happen. And when things don't happen, you harass me in front of my guests, then you drop some kind of excuse like justice. What about justice for us?"

He spoke quickly and downed another cup. I could tell he was getting angry.

"You get all the justice you need with your tax dollars," I said, shrugging. Before he could erupt again, I held up a placating hand. "Ahhh, Yan Tao. You were such a big help to me last time. You got the word out to Duan Cai's group." The last time I passed through, I was on the hunt for Li Ming's lost daughter.[10] We were pressed for time. I was injured. I was cold. I don't recall being very polite. I only feel slightly bad about it.

"The next thing I know, they're all wiped out. Was that you?"

"Me? You think I have nothing better to do than to wipe out a mercenary gang?"

"You have something of a reputation, Magistrate Tao Jun. You leave destruction in your wake."

"Hush, don't use my real name. It's Jin Min. I'm in disguise for a reason."

He gave me a skeptical look, then gestured around at the empty tables beside us. "Fine, 'Mister Jin Min.' You could stand to pick a less conspicuous name."

I nodded appreciatively. "Look, all I wanted was a little chat with Duan Cai's mercenary group. Is it my fault that when I finally found them, they were mostly dead?"

"Well, Duan Cai is not dead. She survived, and she's very angry. I think you finally pushed her over the edge."

"Oh? That's news to me. From what I saw, she didn't know what the edge looked like," I said dryly.

"Yeah, yeah," Yan Tao said dismissively. "Anyway, what do you want?"

I leaned in close, gestured for him to do the same. He eyed me with some suspicion. "Yan Tao, you hear things, right? I was looking for someone, but then they showed up dead. He was muttering something about someone being after him, and he needed help."

"That doesn't sound like something I'd be familiar with."

"His name was Huang Lian."

A flicker of recognition. I'll give Yan Tao some credit, though—he hid it well.

"Nope, never heard of him before."

"Really? Because he had an advertisement for this place. And from what I can tell, he was a regular," I lied about the last part. I didn't know anything about his habits. Sometimes it works. He was quiet for a moment, and he looked like he was either about to cave and tell me what I wanted to know, or he was about to yell at me and tell me to throw myself into the river.

"Come on, Yan Tao. You know something. I'm just trying to figure out what's going on, and why this guy ended up interrupting my lunch and dying on my table." I pulled out a gold ingot from my robe. "Besides, there are certain incentives to talking to me."

He eyed the gold ingot, and I could see the mental math running through that balding head of his. "Ugh, Huang Lian was a regular all right—at least regular enough to pay his tab. Righteous Will Company right? I think the last time I saw him, he was meeting with a pretty boy. Didn't look like a pleasant conversation. Seemed like trouble. There were some angry words."

"What was it about?"

"How am I supposed to know?" Yan Tao muttered angrily. "I try to give my customers privacy, you know? Like a good business."

Out of the corner of my eye, I noticed the young woman, Miao, wiping a table close by. She'd been steadily working her way over to where we were chatting. Yan Tao didn't seem to notice her presence. She seemed to perk up when Yan Tao mentioned the pretty boy.

"What do you know about the Hidden Fist in the area?"

His eyes narrowed. "They're not wanted in this establishment."

"Yan Tao," I warned.

"I'm serious. Look, all I know is that someone was in trouble, and Huang Lian was involved somehow. You're the one that's bringing up assassin sects here. Heaven knows I don't need another huge brawl to break up the place. I finally got the place cleaned up from the last group."

"You've done more than clean up. A whole new addition? And an arena? What changed? This place was kind of a dump before."

Yan Tao stiffened. Whoops. "It wasn't a dump. It just had bad clientele."

"What changed?"

He shrugged. I guess our conversation was over.

"Right," I said, sliding over the gold ingot. He pocketed it. Gave me a curt nod and left.

I poured myself another cup of wine, took a sip and enjoyed the aroma. The restaurant was quiet for the most part —travelers had returned to their rooms, and the locals were making the trip back to the village. Yan Tao's staff began the work of cleaning the place up for the next day.

"You know something, don't you?" I said after Yan Tao walked away. Miao jerked up from the table she was wiping, tried to hide her recognition behind a flinch. "There, you're doing it again. That flinch. You did it earlier when I mentioned the Hidden Fist to Yan Tao. There's no sense in trying to hide it," I said, yawning. "I know what you are. You're all tense—like you're waiting for a fight. You've had some sort of training."

"Mister Jin Min is mistaken," the young woman said.

"Oh, I'm not mistaken," I chuckled. "The thing I don't get is why you're so sloppy."

A tiny flash of a glare spread across her expression, but she controlled it immediately. "I don't know what you mean."

I snatched up the empty wine cup and threw it at her face as hard as I could. Her free arm was there immediately to catch it before it struck her face.

"See? Sloppy. You've shown me that you have some *wugong.*"

"I'm not sloppy. I'm just not hiding it. Everyone here knows what I can do," she explained.

"But they don't know the truth, do they?"

"What truth?"

"You're Hidden Fist, aren't you?"

She shook her head.

"Fine, maybe you are, maybe you aren't. They don't let people just leave. So if you were trained by them and you're still alive, you must have flunked out in a bad way. Incompetence? Do they flunk people for incompetence? I thought they just killed incompetent people."

"I didn't flunk out!"

"Ah," I said, grinning.

She glared. Sometimes it was so easy to get them to spill their secrets. It didn't hurt that she was a little naive. Though a naive assassin was confusing.

"It's okay," I continued. "I just want to help. Look, your

boss trusts me, okay? He provides me information from time to time, and I help keep some of the worst of the bandits away from here."

"There are bandits that still come here."

"I didn't say our arrangement was perfect," I shrugged. She had me there. "If you didn't flunk out, then you're a runaway."

She didn't answer, but I could tell I hit home.

"I'm not a runaway. I earned my freedom."

"I didn't know you could do that." That didn't make any sense. From what I understood, most of the Hidden Fist were raised from a young age to be loyal only to their clan. No one ever ran away or earned their freedom. They either lived as an assassin or died as one. Not much room for personalities or personal preferences there.

"No one has ever done it before."

"But you did?"

She nodded.

"How long ago?"

"A few weeks," she said quietly. She pointed at her arm in the sling. "It wasn't a smooth exit.[11]"

"Does Yan Tao know?"

She shook her head. "I think he suspects. He never asked, though. The less he knows, the better."

I nodded. "Then your secret is safe with me."

She smiled. "I know. I can tell you're honorable."

"You're sure about that? Even after I tricked you into revealing your big secret?" I almost laughed at her. Over the years, I've tried to do more good than bad. But my hands were bloody, and there were hundreds dead because of my choices. Maybe that balances out in life to something called honor. I don't know. I try not to think about it.

"I'm sure."

"You're far too trusting for a former assassin," I chuckled.

"What, did you hit your head or something and lose your memories?"

She stiffened. I must have hit close to home.

"Never mind that. Tell me about Huang Lian of the Righteous Will."

She hesitated, then gave me a single nod. "You're right. He came through here about a week ago. He was supposed to help me with something."

"I was told he was trying to help someone get to safety. Are you the one that someone?" Now we were getting somewhere.

"No," she shook her head.

"Then who is it?"

"It's better that I don't tell you."

"Look, I know you're worried about protecting him and keeping things secret, but Huang Lian is dead."

"What?" She said, the blood drained from her face.

"And right now, you're the only one that knows what he was involved with. Do you know what that means?"

She shook her head. She looked so bewildered. I almost felt sorry for her.

"It means that you're a prime suspect," I said. I pulled out my magistrate's token, set it down deliberately on the table between us. "So tell me this and make it easy on all of us. Are you the one that got him killed?"

"I . . . I. . . . " She stammered.

"Do you know how much trouble you're in?"

"It wasn't me!" the worry on her face was almost heartbreaking. Almost. I don't know if I believed that she was former Hidden Fist, but I had a sense the emotion was real.

"Let's say I believe you," I said. I actually did, but she didn't need to know that. "What was he really trying to help you with? I know he was trying to help someone in danger. What's going on here? It's obviously something worth killing for or else our friend would still be with us."

"I can't tell you."

"You can't or you won't?" I sighed, giving the girl a world-weary smile. "Look kid, I've been in this a long time. Secrets get people killed. It's already gotten your friend killed, and it's probably going to get whoever you're protecting killed as well. Think about that."

She was quiet for a moment, and I figured she was thinking things over in her head. I was almost there, and she was my best lead. I placed the arrow[12] on the table for her to look at. I watched her reaction, caught the slight jerk of her head as she recognized the make. "This is what killed him. You know it, don't you?"

She gave a single nod.

"This is the type of arrow used by the Hidden Fist?"

She blanched but gave a single nod.

"Who are you protecting?" I asked again. She held my gaze for a moment, before abruptly looking to the sword at my side.

"You keep that sword at your side. What is it for?"

"I use it to make sure that people that deserve justice get it."

"Are you a swordsman?"

"I wasn't always a magistrate." I decided to humor her. "In a previous life, I was a swordsman of Blue Mountain."

"Blue Mountain? Like in Old Man Chen's stories?" Her eyes went wide, and she leaned in close. "Are you actually . . . the legendary swordsman Li Ming?"

"There's more than one swordsman of Blue Mountain. I am his sworn brother."

"That's not how the legend goes," she said, looking troubled. "The last swordsman of Blue Mountain is Li Ming. It doesn't say anything about there being more than one swordsman."

"Well it has to say something about a sworn brother right?"

"Uhm . . ."

"Right, so I'm his sworn brother. He's one of the last swordsmen of Blue Mountain. I'm one of the last swordsmen of Blue Mountain. Together, we are the last swordsmen of Blue Mountain."

"Uh-huh," she nodded skeptically.

"Miao! Help me with these guys!" I peeked down to see what Yan Tao was shouting about. Down below by the side of the arena was a pile of bodies that I recognized as the combatants from earlier in the night.

"They're unconscious. Don't worry," Miao said a little too quickly. "At the end of the night, we haul whoever's out cold out onto the street."

My turn to look skeptical. "That's weird."

"Anyway, I've got to get back to work."

I grabbed her arm. "Please. Let me help."

"You want to carry a body?"

"Not that. The other thing."

"Miao!"

"Coming, boss!" She called back.

"They're going to come after you next. I swear on my position as a servant of the emperor, I will not let anything happen to you."

She looked uncertain.

"Fine," I said, also pulling my sword onto the table. "I swear on the grave of my master and my legacy as the last swordsman of Blue Mountain." Technically, it was true—I was a swordsman of Blue Mountain trained in the lost art of the Sword of the Nine Dragons, even if Li Ming went around calling *himself* the last swordsman.

She seemed to accept that one. "I'll come find you in the morning."

"And you'll show me what everyone is after?"

She nodded.

After she made to leave, I rose from my seat as well but

caught a glimpse of the young man down by the stage below. He had his fake beard off by now, and he was staring at Miao as she worked. She smiled that guileless smile at him, and he grinned at her. Was he waiting for her? A rendezvous between young people? They weren't likely to give me any answers, so I left.

4

_____

I should have called that night a win and gone to bed, but my head was filled with a million questions and possibilities. I knew I'd never get to sleep, so I decided to go for a walk.

Miao confirmed our suspicions about the arrow that killed Huang Lian. The Hidden Fist. Assassin sects were something of a grey area for the imperial government. Officially, we were supposed to root them out and arrest everyone associated with them. They were considered to be a 'destabilizing' influence in the empire, and it was my job as a magistrate to take down these groups where possible.

Unofficially? Every governor and major noble house had an assassin clan (or two) in their back pocket to do their dirty work. Just like the criminal underworld, the assassin clans were a crucial part of the *jianghu* economy. This meant that there was a delicate sort of balance when it came to how we were supposed to deal with them. If they drew too much scrutiny, then we were absolutely supposed to step in and take them down. Otherwise, one of the unwritten laws of the kingdom was to turn a blind eye to their doings.

There were rumors that the governor had an assassin sect

in his pocket, though I hadn't uncovered anything yet. It wasn't really my job and business what he did. I knew he was corrupt—we all were. It's a given. The question was always how much could you get away with without drawing attention to yourself. An assassin sect was a good way to keep that attention low. The things I could do with one of my own . . . well, it's nice to dream, right?

I personally didn't have that many interactions with the Hidden Fist, though I knew them by reputation. They were a fearsome bunch. Very professional. Some assassin sects have a tendency to drift into villainy with misplaced plans for domination of the kingdom or whatever nonsense they come up with. Not the Hidden Fist. Everything I ever heard about them was that they did the job they were paid to do and were discrete about it.

There were some things that I just couldn't get my head around. I'd never heard of anyone leaving the Hidden Fist alive. You were either an assassin, or you were dead. There was no other way around it. Most of these assassin clans were like that. Their list of people they've killed would be enough to land them in all kinds of trouble. Add to that how secretive most martial sects are about protecting their *wugong,* and you've got the recipe for instant execution. No survivors.

Except this girl, Miao. It didn't sound like her real name, but that's how she introduced herself, so that was what I was going to stick with. She made it out. I would have expected someone like her to be on the move, trying to stay one step ahead of her pursuers, but the fact that she took a job here at Broken Furniture Inn, one of the most famous inns in the whole *jianghu,* said something otherwise.

She wasn't afraid of the Hidden Fist.

That meant that she was a game changer—someone that disrupted how things ran in the clans. That made her a target, and I knew that if I were the head of an assassin clan, I'd want someone like her removed. Yet, she said she wasn't the one looking to lie low, but she was nervous about something else. What did she get herself involved in?

Either way, it was going to be an interesting visit.

I was so caught up in my thoughts that I didn't notice where I had wandered to. I was some ways down the road from the inn, nearing an octagonal *ting*[1] built near the edge of a cliff of a hill that overlooked the valley below. The moon lit up the storm clouds on the distant horizon, a thin veil over its face. The wind swayed the bamboo trees. The occasional peal of thunder echoed in the distance. I took a deep breath—the suggestion of faraway rain mingled with the early spring chill.

Given how dramatic the weather was, it was no surprise that I should meet someone equally dramatic on the road. As far as mysterious figures went, this one was fairly pedestrian. Black clothes, a black cloth mask, and a cap of black. I meet my fair share of mysterious figures in black in my line of work, and I wish they would wear a different color or something. I suppose it's too much to ask for—an assassin in red wouldn't be so great on anonymity.

"Hello," I called out. "Pleasant evening for a stroll, isn't it?" Sometimes a mysterious figure is just a mysterious figure. No harm, no foul.

They didn't answer.

When they are here to kill you, they usually don't answer. I loosened up my stance, trying not to draw attention to myself. They watched every movement I made but didn't say anything.

"So . . . how about that weather?"

"We sent you a warning," they said. A male voice, from what I could tell. On closer inspection, I could make out a scar that ran down the side of his face.

"I didn't get any warning," I said. "Unless you left it on my desk back in An'lin? Sorry, I'm not at my desk that much. Too much paperwork, and I'm trying to cut back."

"Huang Lian."

"What about him?" I replied, "Oh, you mean that was your warning? A dead body is a pretty dramatic warning."

They didn't answer, but then again, they didn't need to.

"You're meddling in things you don't understand."

"You know, that's the very thing my wife said to me when she kicked me out of the house? And then she said some things that I can't repeat in polite company. Don't worry, she's fine. I'm fine, too. We're working it out. "

"I don't care about your wife."

"Well, good, because I don't care about her either. And it would be really weird if you did."

They clenched their fist. I could tell I was getting to them. It's another trick I've learned over the years. Babble. Yep. That's the trick. If everyone thinks you're an idiot because of all the nonsense you're spewing, then they're going to underestimate you. Or you might make them angry, and they'll make a mistake. Either way, they'll be off balance, and that's when you strike. And that's not something they'll teach you at a martial arts sect.

I kept going. "So you're an archer, are you? We don't see a lot of that type in the *jianghu*. Not much for martial arts when you've got a bow. But I suppose if you're an assassin, that makes sense. Just hide somewhere far away and hit them with an arrow. A coward's way to fight."

They didn't respond, staying as stoic as ever. It didn't get the reaction I was looking for. I decided to try a different approach. "So what are you? Hidden Fist? I've seen your kind flitting around before. Always some kind of sneaky dark thing to do. Makes you look so self-important. I would know. I'm a magistrate, so I know all about self-important displays."

"You've been warned. Stay away. You're not going to get a second chance."

"You know, if you hadn't killed him, I probably wouldn't have come out here?" I lied. "But a murder and then a death threat by this beautiful pavilion on a stormy night like this? That's practically an open invitation to keep poking at things I don't understand."

"Just stay away."

"Stay away from what? You need to be a little more specific in your warnings."

"Stay away."

"Or what?" I said. I probably shouldn't have. But they were annoying me, and I was getting to be in a bad mood.

They threw a short throwing knife they kept at their waist, but I was a hair faster. I unsheathed Joy and knocked it out of the air. The white steel of my blade practically glowed in the moonlight. It's moments like this that I really appreciate how beautiful the weapon is[2]. I would have spent a moment admiring it, but hey, I had someone to deal with.

Joy felt comfortable in my hand, like a reunion with an old friend on a warm summer dusk. I span my sword around in a flourish, and then kicked off my back foot in a fast lunge. I wasn't quick enough. The assassin had enough time to draw his short sword (more of a long dagger) that he held in a backhand grip. I pushed my advantage with a flurry of strikes, but he was fast enough to meet each attack. His open hand struck out at my chest, and I twisted to avoid the blow.

The assassin used the moment to kick up the pillars of the *ting* and flip up onto the tiled roof, his feet landing on the upturned corner of the eaves.

I disengaged, using my qinggong to gain some distance between us. I considered my opponent. He was good, but I was pretty confident that I could take him. Then again, he was on the roof and had the higher ground…[3]

"Are we going to make a thing out of this?" I asked.

"Even if you kill me, more will come."

"Am I supposed to be scared off by that?" In my hands, Joy felt eager for a fight. At this point in the night, I wasn't above getting my hands dirty.

"Killing a magistrate is not in our plans," they said. "But it can be. Consider this your final warning."

He turned, and with an admittedly graceful flip, leaped from the *ting* and over the edge of the cliff. Sure, it sounds dramatic, but it wasn't that far down. I didn't bother to give chase. For one, I'm too old for that kind of crap. And don't tell me about those storytellers that spin a tale of eighty-year-old Five Foot Chou or whoever and how their qinggong practically let them fly. Like I said, qinggong was not my strength, and I wasn't about to go chasing after someone through the trees. The other reason was simple. I was tired, and I wanted to go to bed and I had a long walk ahead of me to get back to the inn. Besides, I had no doubt I'd see him again and that our third encounter would be our last.

5

I WOKE UP BLEARY-EYED AND GROGGY FROM LACK OF SLEEP. Ji Ping, who didn't have any nighttime adventures, was bright-eyed and ready for the day. He somehow managed to find time to shave too. Officer Ruo, I could tell, was nursing a light hangover. Every time Ji Ping said something, he winced a little more than usual.

I held a hand up to the window, trying to block out the light. It spilled through my outstretched fingers. I yawned, contorting my face into a look of general disgust about being awake. Ji Ping took this as a sign to come over and further rouse me.

"Good morning, Magistrate," he greeted with a slight bow. His cheeriness was going to be a problem. "How did you sleep?"

"Uggggh," I groaned.

"Come on, Magistrate, we have work to do."

"I did that last night. Let me sleep in."

"How would that look? A magistrate sleeping in? What would the people say?"

"We're in disguise. No one knows I'm a magistrate here." I said, groaning again. But he had done it. I was awake. He always knew what to do to get me going for the day. I suppose it's why I liked keeping him around. He helps me be productive, otherwise all I'd do is sleep.

You can never get enough sleep.

There was a knock on the door. Officer Ruo reached for his dagger, took up position by the side of the door. We weren't expecting trouble, but it didn't hurt to be safe. I nodded at Ji Ping, who clicked his tongue in disapproval about being ordered around but opened the door.

Miao stood there and greeted us with that guileless smile. The young woman stepped around Ji Ping, gave Ruo a slightly amused smile. I waved a hand at Ruo to stand down. Puzzled, he put his knife away.

"What's the meaning of this, young lady?" Ji Ping asked.

"Hush, Ji Ping, it's ok. This is my new friend, Miao."

"Good morning, Mister Jin Min," she said, bowing.

Immediately, Ruo and Ji Ping snickered.

"What's so funny?" I said.

"Jin Min? Like the famous singer?" Ruo asked.

"Is this why our magistrate comes in so tired? Is he out there serenading the women?" Ji Ping asked.

"He must not have very much luck if he keeps hanging around us!"

They burst into laughter again. This time, Miao even joined in with a snicker.

"I am Mr. Jin Min," I said, annoyed. "Anyway, what is it Miao?"

"I thought I could take you to . . . what we discussed yesterday."

"Oh, how mysterious," said Ji Ping.

"Probably a poetry recital," Ruo said, and they burst out laughing again.

"Come on . . . lead the way," I grumbled.

"Yes, master Jin Min," Miao said, giggling.

Sometimes I hate everyone.

It was a fifteen-minute walk down the road from the inn and into Yuan'Men. I liked the town. Every time I passed through it, I had the thought that it might be nice to retire here one day. Beautiful woods, proximity to the Kuan river, and a stunning view of the mountains—all the stuff of poets. The settlement straddled that awkward phase between town and village—it had more people and commerce than a village, but it didn't quite have the right numbers to be a full-fledged town. Nevertheless, there was a thriving economy here. Around the main market and the central hubs of the town, a few two-story buildings had taken root. And if there's anything I know about towns, it's that buildings get bigger and taller the more prosperous the town gets.

I knew the local officials, and normally I would have, *should* have, paid my respects, and then requisitioned their help in the case, but I was traveling in disguise. When we arrived, the storm clouds were growing thicker. I frowned up at the weather and the distant peal of thunder. We walked through a world of stark opposites. The bright light of the sun was a poignant contrast to the dark clouds of the encroaching storm.

We heard the noise of the performance troupe before we saw it. A cacophony of music, cheering, and the ringing crash of bos[1]. What would normally have been the center of town had turned into a fair of sorts. Four stages were constructed in the center, a giant banner behind the main stage with the words, "THE MAGNIFICENT SHOW" in bold print. Another banner to the side of the stage bore the Cyclone Defenders' name. A pair of poles on opposite ends of the square with a rope suspended between them. Two jugglers were on the main stage, tossing eight jugs back and forth in a series of increasingly complex patterns. Some damn fool drinking fuel and blowing fire.

It was a real variety show.

I looked around for animals. I liked seeing the animals. But to my disappointment, there were no animals.

"The acrobatic troupe?" I asked Miao. "They were at the inn last night."

She nodded. "They got here two weeks ago. They perform at the inn for some free publicity."

"I wish we had more time off to come to these things," Ruo complained. "We never get time off, and they never come to the city."

"They don't come to the city because they don't want to pay the taxes in An'lin," Ji Ping explained. It made sense. No one wanted to run afoul of An'lin's taxes. That's why the towns of An'Zhao and He'bian are so prosperous. But I suppose less money for An'lin means less money for government officials. Not that it mattered. I was wealthy enough—it helps having a rich family—but I knew it made a difference to some of my other magistrate peers. They liked to skim a little off the top after giving the emperor his due. I didn't really care for that. I didn't need it, and people suffer enough under the emperor's rule as it was.

There was little thought of taxes today at the variety show. It was full of life and energy in a way that I hadn't seen in the years since the war. A young father carried his son on his shoulders, and it reminded me of a distant memory of my father taking me and his other sons on a trip to somewhere, and our caravan passed through a town where a menagerie was happening. I pleaded with him to let me see it, and he indulged me and called the caravan to halt for the day. It was probably one of the best days of my life, and I even got to pet a leopard. I spared a thought for my father, somewhere with our ancestral holdings in the capital. He was a high-ranking official these days and had no time for menageries.

I wondered if my own son would want to go to a menagerie. I felt a small pang of guilt that I didn't know.

Miao lead us to the edge of the square, and I took in the sights. The square was packed with people from all over. I saw a few monks from the Mountain River Monastery[2], with their distinctly shaved heads. I made eye contact with one of them, and he eyed me with some suspicion. I turned away from them before they could recognize me—disguise or no. I didn't want any more trouble. More than a handful of northerners, enjoying the turn of the seasons, traveling south. And villagers, and even some of the idle rich of An'lin, had ventured out to the menagerie.

"So where is this person that you're helping?"

"It won't be long now," she said. There was something off about her tone. I couldn't tell what it was exactly, but I had a suspicion. I needed to know more about this girl. Somehow, all of this centered around her, and while her own hands may or may not be clean, people had already died because of her involvement.

"So, tell me about your time in the Hidden Fist," I asked as we approached the edge of the crowd.

She shook her head. "I don't fully remember."

"You don't remember?" I frowned.

She shook her head again.

"I find that hard to believe."

"I lost my memories. For a long time, I didn't know who I was. I didn't even know I could fight," she replied. "So when you said something about hitting my head . . ."

"That was a joke."

"But one that hit close to the truth. I had no recollection of anything. My head hurt, and I was hungry, and I had the bad luck to run into bandits."

"And then your body moved on its own."

She nodded. "You get it, don't you? You're a swordsman. Sometimes you just act without thinking."

That was why we trained and trained and trained and trained, and when we were tired, we trained some more. It took too long to think. When your life is in danger, the only thing you can really do is act and trust in your training. Thinking about it too much would likely bring disaster.

"That must have been disconcerting."

"I was scared. I didn't know who I was or why I had these skills. Lucky for me, I found Yan Tao."

"That's how you ended up at Broken Furniture Inn," I said. At least that part of her story made sense. Whatever else Yan Tao was, he did have a good heart. "He took you in?"

"Green Brocade Inn," she corrected. "He gave me something to eat. You know how it is at Green Brocade—it wasn't long until a fight broke out. He gave me a job after I dealt with some unruly customers," she met my gaze. "He saved me."

"Some of your memories have come back."

"I only have fragments. They feel like half remembered dreams. I don't remember specifics of what I used to do as a Hidden Fist or even who I was back then. Sometimes it feels like I'm looking at a dirty mirror, and I see someone that I don't recognize. Whoever that was, whoever I used to be, scares me. I don't want anything to do with it. Do you think it's possible?"

Was it possible to run away from your past? I thought about Master Guo, the years Li Ming and I spent hunting our master's killer. The Black Tiger rebellion threatening to rip the empire apart once again. The sins of the past inevitably become the worries of the future.

I didn't think it was possible to escape your past.

"Yes," I lied.

She smiled at me. She seemed to accept my answer.

We stood near the edge of the crowd, not wanting to work our way in any closer. Officer Ruo, on the other hand, barged his way into the audience, using his size like a battering ram. Ji Ping stayed close in his shadow, enjoying the path the large man cleared for him. I didn't bother to tell them we weren't here to sightsee, rolling my eyes at their behavior. Why did I even bring them along on investigations?

Because Ji Ping would track me down otherwise, and I would never hear the end of it, I remembered. For all their lack of social skills, their combined tracking prowess was truly impressive. At times, it reminded me that I was under as much supervision as a prisoner.

I sighed.

"There," Miao pointed. "The one on the stage right now. His name is Dong Jiang."

I looked up and saw who she was talking about, and it all made sense. It was the young man from yesterday—General Chao with the fake beard. Up close, the young man was even better looking. Dong Jiang had the kind of face that both men and women gasped over, like "Wow, that's a very handsome man." It's the kind of face that you wish you never saw because you would curse the heavens that you were born looking like a goat. He wore his hair in a small topknot and the rest billowed down past his shoulders. He had a warm smile that he raked across the crowd. The young women up front swooned. Even Miao beside me stirred.

"He's the one in danger?" I asked.

She nodded. "Dong Jiang has been visiting the inn fairly frequently—even when the troupe wasn't performing there. He was always friendly and fun to talk to, so I got to know him a little better. About a week ago, he looked troubled, and he told me that he was in danger."

"And you believed him?"

She nodded. "Why wouldn't I?"

Inwardly, I groaned. So, she was a little on the naive side.

"But he's right, isn't he?" she asked. "I mean, if Huang Lian is dead, then there must be a real threat."

She had me there.

"You've been a lovely audience," Dong Jiang said, spreading his arms wide to the crowd. "We have a special treat for you—a new performance we haven't shown anyone else before. And now we bring you the famous sword duel of the three Lords of Sen'lin. Not too long ago, the paths of three masters of the *wu'lin* intersected by a well-known inn. They had heard of each other's fame and decided to test each other's skills in a friendly three way match."

The young man flourished a metal fan as two more men joined him on the stage. They wore sleeveless shirts, one with an open vest that showed his chest and abdomen. Apparently, the early spring chill didn't bother them. The first carried a pair of hook swords. The other, a set of crescent moon knives. Impressive weapons—especially for performers.

"They're assassins," Miao explained.

"Which ones?"

"The two of them."

"You recognize them?"

She turned pale and shook her head. "They're both Hidden Fist, though."

"How can you tell?"

"See the way he holds the crescent moon knives? That's something that Shifu Master Chen Gao would beat into us. They weren't a part of the troop three days ago," she shuddered from the recollection.

"Are they here for you?"

"I don't think so," she said.

"How do you know?"

"They would have made a move on me already," she replied, nodding towards her arm in the sling. "I'm an easy target with my injury."

"So they're after him?"

She nodded. I kept my hand close to my sword at my side, in case I needed to intervene.

A musician rang the gong, and an old man on the erhu began playing a warbling melody accompanied by a young woman on a flute. The crowd cheered as the three performers settled into stances and began their choreographed performance.

It began slowly, with the three performers first circling to the left and then back to the right. They raised their weapons to the sky and then brushed it close to the earth. Then their weapons slowly became part of the performance, with each man flashing their weapons to the crowd as they moved to the tempo. It was a fine piece of artistry—I would never have guessed that the two assassins were not performers, and the young man with the fan seemed like a natural on stage.

Each had their moment on stage, showcasing their movements. Dong Jiang struck left with the fan, then towards the crowd, and then backflipped to the crowd's approval. Then came the one with the hook swords. In a flurry of strikes, he connected his blades together and swung them over his head before disconnecting them and landing in a split. The third, with the crescent moon knives, was the most acrobatic of them all. His display was a series of flips, kicks, and turns that culminated in an impressive jumping split leg kick.

Yet, the more I watched the performance, the more I worried about Miao. She was entranced by the fight, the same way as everyone else, which made me curious. If she really were Hidden Fist, she would have seen much better fights. And if she were working at the Broken Furniture Inn, then she was probably involved with much better fights.

The tempo *bo* crashed, and the heavy thumping of drums edged the *erhu* and flute into a faster melody. The duel began in earnest. As with any three-way fight, this one began with a note of chaos. Attacking and defending all done in unison. With one stroke of an attack, the second stroke a defense. Where two combined to attack one, their fortunes changed quickly as openings formed.

It was a good performance, though the proximity of the blades slashing by the young man with the fan gradually became more alarming. The audience, believing the danger to be part of the show, cheered louder and louder. Beside me, Miao stiffened a little in worry but joined in the cheering by raising her non-sling arm in the air.

Oh no. I realized. *She's in love with him.*

Or just infatuated. I couldn't tell. The line between swooning and thirsting was so very fine.

Despite her ease and enjoyment, there were little things she did that caught my attention: the way she still unconsciously looked over her shoulder, scanned the environment for threats. Everything was still a little fresh. That meant she wasn't too far removed from her time as an assassin.

It would be a mistake to let her get involved again.

By the way she looked up at the stage at the trio of men performing their elaborate routine . . .

I groaned inwardly at the things that I would have to do. I grabbed her arm, and she looked up at me in alarm. "Does pretty boy know you were formerly Hidden Fist?"

"Yes," she said.

"Why did you tell him?"

She shrugged.

Damn.

"And the other assassins?"

"I've never met them before. They're new here."

"The only other person that knows your secret is me?"

"Just you."

I let go of her arm, and she rubbed where I grabbed gingerly. She wasn't in trouble. At least not yet, though I couldn't be sure what pretty boy would do with that information.

The musicians brought the melody up to a fever pitch, the erhu singing in the highest tones. And as the performance continued, the weapons began crossing dangerously close to each of the performers' vital parts. A stab of the hook blades passed just under the armpit of the young man with a fan. Then came a slash of the crescent moon blades that he barely had time to duck under. With the final crash of drums, he twisted away from another cut, but this one left the young man with a faint line of red on his neck. He glared at his other performers and they bowed to the roaring crowd.

A performance accident. A great way to mask a murder.

Master Lei ascended the stage, his gaudy coat billowing behind him. "Thank you! Thank you!" He shouted with an unnecessary flourish of his cape. "Our performers will be taking a short half hour break. In the meantime, you'll notice some of the performers will be mingling among you with baskets. Please make a donation if you can. Your support makes our show possible!"

"Come on, I'll take you to meet Dong Jiang," Miao said. She lead me around to the back of the stage. There were other young women there, clearly waiting to get a glimpse of the handsome performer. They glared as we walked past. And I heard their whispers and the cruel things they were saying about Miao. If their comments bothered her, she didn't show it, though I will admit that as far as insults go, they were pretty pedestrian, and not worth the time.

The young man waved when he saw Miao approaching, though he gave me an uncertain and suspicious look. He hefted a jar of *huangjiu,*[3] and took a long sip from it.

A little early in the day to be drinking like that, I thought.

"Miao!" the young man called out and hurried to her side. He dabbed a cloth at the cut on his neck. Up close, he looked to be a couple of years older than Miao—still painfully young to be mixed up in something so dangerous. "I'm so glad you came to the show. Did Yan Tao give you the morning off?"

Miao nodded, and the young man immediately gave her a warm embrace. I raised an eyebrow. I wasn't much for propriety, but he seemed pretty brazen, and his hands lingered in places that spoke of ulterior motives.

I already didn't like him.

She flushed from the display of public affection. "Dong Jiang, I want you to meet Mister Jin Min. He's the one I told you about."

"The swordsman of Blue Mountain? The honor is mine, Mister Jin Min," he said, cupping his fist and bowing in the manner of the *jianghu*. A swordsman, huh? Is that what Miao told the young man about me? I could use that.

I returned the salute. "I understand that you're in trouble, Dong Jiang."

The young man's eyes narrowed as he sized me up, then looked to Miao. "You really think he can help us?"

She nodded. "Huang Lian is dead, Dong Jiang."

"What?" he said, his face turning pale. "When did this happen?"

"Two days ago in An'lin," I said. "He came to me for help. Told me to come looking for you two. Whoever is after you means business."

I wondered if he would pick up on the lie. He frowned slightly, but nodded.

"Why don't you tell me what's going on?"

He looked around at the crowd, the line of admirers hoping to meet him. "I'll tell you later. There's too many people around."

"Look, people are after you, and I don't want to stick my neck out for you unless I know what's going on. So, you better start talking soon," I said gruffly, trying to give my best Li Ming impression. "Give me the short version."

"People want to kill me."

"A bit more than that," I growled.

"The Hidden Fist are after him," Miao added, trying to soothe things between us.

"And why are they after you?"

"I don't know. Isn't it enough that they want to kill me?"

"Well, you know what, I don't remember how to use a sword anymore," I said, turning to walk away.

"Wait, wait, Mister Jin Min, please," Miao said. "We really need your help."

"Fine, only because the young lady said so," I said, playing along.

"They're already here for me! They haven't killed me yet because they're hoping to take me alive. But they're here!"

"Suppose I believe you. What do you need?"

"I—we—need somewhere to lie low. Maybe somewhere out of the province," the young man said.

"We?" I asked, glancing at Miao. She didn't meet my gaze. "Fine, somewhere to lay low. I know some people that can smuggle you out. But it'll take some time. A couple of days . . ."

"We don't have that much time!" Dong Jiang said, removing the cloth from his neck. "They're going to kill me! Today's performance was clearly a warning!"

"Or you were just clumsy."

"You!"

"I thought you said they wanted to capture you. Now you're saying they want to kill you? Which is it?"

"Dong Jiang . . ." Miao said. "It'll be okay. Mister Jin Min can help us."

Dong Jiang sighed, "Look, I need to get back on stage soon. We can talk more after the show." He waved at the line of fans, then climbed up the steps to the stage.

"I'm sorry. That didn't go well," Miao said as we walked back to the audience. "I hope you'll still consider helping us."

"It's okay. I'll do what I can."

There was something off about this. Miao seemed on the level. But Dong Jiang? I didn't trust him.

I looked back over my shoulder at the young man. He was drinking out of the jar of huangjiu again.

"A little early in the day for him to be drinking like that, isn't it?"

"It's his favorite drink," she shrugged. "He loves huangjiu."

"And you know his favorite drink? Just how close are you?"

She shrugged again.

———

The performer with the hook blades stood at the base of one of the tall poles. With a flourish of his hands, he scaled the pole in three fluid kicks—showing off some of his qinggong. The crowd cheered.

He carried a bow up with him, and his companion, the performer with the crescent moon blades, tossed arrows up for him to catch. The crowd cheered their approval. Perched on the rope with just his toes, he readied his bow to fire at a row of targets across the square.

An archer.

My mind raced with a hundred thoughts as the pieces of the case started fitting together. Archer. Assassins. Was this my friend from the restaurant? Was he the one that paid me a visit last night? If what Miao said was true, then this was our murderer—an assassin from the Hidden Fist.

I should have arrested him then and there. But I didn't. I own this mistake. If I had acted, then maybe things wouldn't have been so complicated later. Or maybe it would have been more complicated? I don't know. I'm not a fortune teller, and the whims of the gods are a mystery to me. All I know is that I was distracted by a jostling in the crowd as Ruo and Ji Ping pushed their way back to my side.

"Magistrate!" Ji Ping exclaimed. I hissed. Someone turned to see what the commotion was about.

"Shhhh, not so loud!"

"Magistrate, a word?" He whispered.

"Magistrate? What magistrate? I'm Mister Jin Min."

"The famous singer?" someone murmured.

I grabbed Ji Ping and pulled him aside. Miao was engrossed in the next performance and didn't notice.

"What is it?" I whispered Ji Ping.

"It's the guy! It's the guy!"

"Calm down, Ji Ping. What guy?"

"I am calm!" he said angrily. "Anyway, the one with the fan? I recognize his face."

"The pretty one?"

He frowned. "I guess he's pretty."

If it was anyone else, I'd say they were full of it. But Ji Ping has a tendency to be right about these sorts of things. I usually don't need to check the records because Ji Ping already knows it. Sometimes I wonder that *he's* not the magistrate instead of me. Thank you, father for a political appointment, I guess.

"I couldn't tell last night—we were too far away. But I got a good look at his face today, and I'm sure of it. His real name is Pian Ren. He's wanted in three provinces."

"Oh?"

"He's the one in the bulletin, wanted in connection to the fireworks factory destruction in Tu'men."

"You're certain?" my eyes widened. This was a stroke of good luck for us. "Did the bulletin say anything else about him?"

Ji Ping squinted his eyes shut as he recalled what he could about Pian Ren. "He charms unsuspecting people, robs them of their money, and then gambles it all away."

"A minor criminal?" Minor could be an understatement. Those with gambling debts were capable of incredible acts of stupidity and harm.

"Well, that's not the worst of it. He's also responsible for the deaths of over fifty people."

"Oh. Well, that's different."

"He was involved in a confrontation with four other men at the fireworks factory in Tu'men. A witness said he sabotaged the factory and used the chaos to escape. I guess he ran here."

I sighed. "You couldn't have told me this a few minutes ago?"

"Magistrate?"

"I just talked to him a few moments ago. If I had known he was a person of interest, I would have arrested him on the spot." I shook my head.

"I was looking for you, Magistrate, but you pulled one of your disappearing tricks again," Ji Ping said testily.

I sighed again. "Never mind. Did your bulletin say anything about how he pissed off the Hidden Fist?"

Ji Ping looked surprised. "The Hidden Fist?"

I nodded at the performer, now at the top of the pole. "Do you recognize him?"

Ji Ping shook his head.

"Well, according to our source here," I gestured towards Miao, "they're both assassins from the Hidden Fist. And they want to kill him."

"The Hidden Fist?" Ji Ping gasped. "Should we arrest them?"

"Not yet." I shook my head. "I want to see how things play out."

"But what if they kill him?"

I shrugged. "Then our problems have been solved."

"You're a bad man, Magistrate," Ji Ping frowned.

"I know."

Suddenly, everything happened at once. There was a loud twanging noise, followed by a cry of fear. I looked up to see the end of the tightrope twisting through the air like an angry snake. A moment later, a heavy thud on the square, and then came the screaming of the crowd.

Ji Ping and I exchanged a quick glance, and we hurried to where the crowd was hurrying (and in most cases, running) away. I checked behind me to make sure Miao was following along as we pushed our way through the crowd, swimming upstream. I couldn't find her. I cursed and kept going. Some men and women had fainted, while others fanned themselves from the shock.

"Get out of the way! Make way!" We pushed our way through the crowd. I used my elbows where I could, shoving people aside. A heavy hand fell on my shoulder, and I looked up to see Officer Ruo push me behind him.

"MOVE!" He bellowed.

The crowd parted.

Miao was somehow already there at the body's side.

The performer's head was a bloody mess. His face smashed in and blood splattered everywhere. His arm twisted in a way that looked completely wrong—likely from when he tried to break his fall.

But how does someone skilled in qinggong fall to their death? I examined his legs. There was no obvious sign of severed tendons or anything. No overt wounds to the abdomen to disrupt the flow of qi. Besides, he was just doing the performance on the stage, and he seemed fine. He even scaled the pole just fine.

I leaned over the corpse, sniffing the mess of the ruined face. Under the scent of blood, I caught a hint of something vaguely familiar. A floral scent, sweet like Jasmine, but like the dark side of a flower scorned.

The poison of Qiang Ge's Tears?

I couldn't tell for sure, but it was a relatively easy poison to make, if you knew what you were doing, and one that specifically disrupted the flow of qi. The ingredients were rare, but given its properties, I wondered why people didn't use it more often.

Easier to just kill a man the normal way.

Was there a connection here to the Treasury robbery? I sighed. Too many questions and variables. Not enough facts. Not yet.

"I don't see any signs of darts or needles," Miao confirmed. "Nothing that could have knocked him off the rope."

I knelt down next to the body. There wasn't much left of his face, but I recognized the scar on his chin. Not very many people could have had such a nasty, gnarly looking scar.

My archer friend from the night before.

This was getting complicated.

"Magistrate Tao Jun. Trouble just follows you everywhere you go, doesn't it?" A woman's voice said from across me. I looked up from the corpse to find Jingyi looming over me. "And don't you have a case to solve?"

"Things were going just fine until you showed up," I retorted.

"If this is just fine, I'd hate to see a disaster," Jingyi said, gesturing to the corpse.

"What are you doing here, Jingyi?"

"What am I doing here? I told you I was coming out here to help with the investigation."

Before I could answer, Mayor Qiao, one of the local officials I had been avoiding, blurted out, "Magistrate Tao Jun! Magistrate Tao Jun! I'm so glad you're here . . ."

So much for traveling in disguise.

" . . . A death! You have to understand, magistrate, this isn't my fault."

I fought the urge to roll my eyes. It hadn't even been five minutes, and he was already trying to shift the blame to someone else.

"Miao, what are you doing here?" Jingyi asked.

"Hello, Mistress Jingyi," Miao said with a little wave.

"You two know each other?" These things shouldn't surprise me, but they did.

"We've met a few times," Jingyi said.

The crowd started murmuring again with worry. I pulled out my magistrate's seal and yanked Mayor Qiao over by the hem of his robe. He squirmed under my grip. "We need to get these people out of here so we can examine the body."

"Uh . . . yes, Magistrate!" Mayor Qiao said without moving.

"Well? Go on!" I all but yelled at him.

"Attention! Attention! Please leave the area in an orderly fashion!"

When no one would move, Officer Ruo bellowed again. "LEAVE!"

The crowd gathered around the body slowly began to disperse.

"Well, you'll be glad to know I solved the murder of Huang Lian," I said, rising from the side of the corpse.

"You did? Who was it?"

I nodded down at the dead body.

"This guy?"

"He was an assassin from the Hidden Fist. Miao said—"

"Wait, where did Miao go?" Jingyi interrupted.

I looked around. She wasn't on the stage, and the crowd was too thick to find her. There was no sign of Dong Jiang, or whatever his name was, either. I cursed.

"Ruo, Ji Ping, find that performer," I ordered. Officer Ruo saluted and pushed people aside as he cut through the crowd. "Mistress Bai, would you be so kind as to find Miao?"

"You think she's involved in this?" Jingyi asked, puzzled. "She's just a girl."

"Oh, she's definitely more than that." I grimaced. "I don't know how exactly, but she's involved in all of this."

6

THE FIRST DISAPPOINTMENT OF THE DAY WAS THAT THEY DIDN'T find Pretty Boy Pian Ren, or Dong Jiang, or whatever his name was. What they did find was a giant headache.

For me.

It took me a good three hours to lose the officials and their pleas. Between their sycophantic bowing and scraping and cries for clemency, and their constant presence, I was pretty sure they were hiding something. I suspected it wasn't too dangerous—maybe a kickback or two from the performance troupe. But there were layers of guilt that I had to wade through that I wasn't interested in dealing with today.

It also took me another hour to deal with the bureaucratic storm that followed. I was lucky Ji Ping was there to help. Ji Ping talked to the local clerk, and they sequestered themselves in a record room for some time.

To make matters worse, it would take more than a day for a coroner to come out to Yuan'men and investigate the body. It wasn't fast enough. There was an urgency here that no one else understood. I knew that by the time the coroner arrived, whatever was going to happen would have already happened. Ji Ping and I poured over the body ourselves, though our inspections turned up scant new information.

Our interviews of the members of the Cyclone Defenders also yielded few results. The dead man was the hook blade wielding performer named Zhang Yuanjun. He kept to himself, and despite how close the rest of the Cyclone Defenders were to each other, they didn't know much about him. He was supposedly the brother of Zhang Yuanhai, the performer who used the crescent moon blades. Conveniently enough for them, Yuanhai was nowhere to be found either. That wasn't surprising. If my 'brother' had been killed earlier in the day, I'd go to ground too.

When the final pieces of the day had finally settled, I walked the path back to the inn, my mood foul. The inn was as lively as it was last night. There were no sign of any performers from the Cyclone Defenders' troupe, though that didn't seem to stop the popularity of the arena. Two bare-chested men grappled with each other, much to the delight of the crowd.

The second disappointment was that Miao was nowhere to be seen tonight, which set me in a bit worse of a mood because I had a whole list of questions for her. I asked Yan Tao if he had seen her and he shrugged.

"She can take care of herself," he said.

"I'm sure she can, but she's still in danger."

"She can take care of herself," he said more firmly, despite the concern entering his eyes.

Instead, I settled into my table from the night before. A serving boy brought me a plate of bao, and I sipped some tea while stewing over the day's events.

The murder of Huang Lian was more or less solved—the archer that killed him was now a corpse in Yuan'men. But the motivation of the Hidden Fist still eluded me. The pretty boy, Dong Jiang, said the assassins were here to take him in alive.

The Hidden Fist went so far as to kill Huang Lian and trap him. And while Dong Jiang and Miao were nowhere to be found, it meant that I still had a bit of time. Somehow, an assassin that skilled in archery and *qinggong* was dead. It didn't take a magistrate to know that it was murder. But how did Miao fit in with all of this?

Given her past, it wasn't too much of a leap to imagine her murdering the assassins that were trying to kill Pretty Boy. She was the obvious culprit, but perhaps a bit too obvious. But my instincts said she wasn't responsible for their deaths. I'm usually a pretty good read of people, and despite her upbringing, I didn't think she was responsible for the performer's death.

No, there was something else going on here, and a lot of dead people for just a simple con man. Something still wasn't making sense, and I couldn't quite put my finger on it.

There are moments when nothing makes sense, and the best thing I've found that you can do in those moments is to just call it a day. I retired to my room early, leaving behind the cheering of the arena.

The third disappointment of the night was that I didn't get more than two hours of sleep before there came a pounding on my door. Having already dealt with two dead bodies in the course of two days, it really shouldn't have surprised me when I was called out to the acrobatic troupe for yet another dead body. I woke to someone calling my name through the door and pounding on the doorframe. When I slid the door open, I was greeted by Jingyi who was already dressed and held a paper lantern, ready to go.

"What's going on?"

"Another dead body. Let's go," she said.

"That's not how this works," I grumbled.

I did not appreciate having to go in the middle of the night. That sort of thing is for young people. Or assassins. Or thugs. Or even my own officers. I'm not the one that should have to get hauled out of bed. Nevertheless, I followed Jingyi out. Ji Ping and Ruo were already waiting outside. Ji Ping wore a mask of anxiety, while Ruo had that same sleepy expression he always had.

Miao was still nowhere to be seen, and no one knew where she was. I admit, I was starting to get worried.

When we arrived, the square was quiet, and only a handful of people were out. Mayor Qiao stood around looking worried while chatting with a grimacing Master Lei, the troupe leader. He had a desperate pleading in his eyes that I tried to ignore. I didn't have time to deal with him. Master Lei, on the other hand, looked defeated. Without his gaudy cape, the man seemed smaller, like the troubles of the entire world fell on his shoulders in a single night. The other performers were huddled around, speaking in hushed whispers. Some of them I recognized from earlier in the day. Small groups of women and men were crying, cursing. Someone muttered something about bad luck, and ancestors, and leaving before things got worse.

I had a feeling I knew who was dead.

It was probably the second Hidden Fist assassin.

I sighed, thinking about the amount of paperwork I'd have to do.[1]

"Magistrate Tao Jun," Master Lei said. "Please, come this way."

Master Lei waved me into a tent where they found the dead body. I entered, Ji Ping and Jingyi close behind. Ji Ping gave Jingyi an uncertain look—I knew he didn't really trust the *jianghu* type, but I didn't feel like explaining her presence.

The dead man slumped against a crate that doubled as an eating table. A half-eaten bao like an empty promise sat next to a spilled jar of wine, its contents dripping down the side of the crate.

I squatted down next to the body, checking for any obvious wounds. Jingyi held the lantern close as I looked, and I nodded my thanks. No fatal strikes to the *dantian*[2] No puncture wounds on this one either. No needles, darts, or anything like that.

My best guess, like the other death earlier today, was poison. I sniffed the wine, flinching at the sharp vinegar and fermented fruity scent of the huangjiiu. But underneath that, I caught the scent of something else.

Qiang Ge's Tears. The same poison thought to be used in the attack on the treasury envoys. I was sure of it this time.

How interesting.

Two men dying in the same day to the same kind of poison? This wasn't a coincidence. The pieces started coming together in my head. Nothing concrete—it still needed time to cook—but I could feel it. We were close to figuring out how this all tied together.

The smell of the wine and the poison brought my mind back to a distant memory at Blue Mountain Pavilion. It was a rare lesson from Old man Ye. His skill was in alchemy and medicine, the blending of different herbs together to boost the ability to cultivate our qi. He was showing us disciples the different combinations of herbs and the effect they could have on the body.

"Some of these herbs are not potent enough on their own," he had said. "They need a catalyst to boost their strength. In fact, without the catalyst, you'll reap no benefit from it."

He handed us a pair of flowers to examine.

"The same is true of poison," he said, holding up the pistil of a flower. "On its own, Qiang Ge's tears will disrupt the flow of qi, but combined with the right elements, it will kill a man. It all depends on the type of *jiu*[3]. Dry jiu won't work, but fruity jiu will turn Qiang Ge's Tears into a potent weapon."

He poured a cup of *jiu* and then added a few drops from a vial he kept in his robe. Then he took a sniff of it and nodded grimly. He passed the cup to us, indicating that we should sniff as well. "Remember this smell. If you detect it, don't drink. This will save your life."

Old man Ye wasn't the nicest of teachers, and I don't think the others were listening. But I hung onto every word, fascinated. It seemed to me like it was cheating—a shortcut to a higher level of cultivation—and I wanted to know more.

Unfortunately, he wasn't the type to share his secrets, but still the lesson remained. I moved to the spilled jar of wine. It looked similar to the type of wine Dong Jiang was drinking earlier in the day.

I looked around the tent. In the corner of the tent, Ji Ping was examining a pair of crescent moon blades. Just as I suspected. This was the other assassin.

"This was Zhang Yuanhai," Master Lei said. "He was the brother of Zhang Yuanjun, the performer that fell earlier today. He must have been so distraught over his brother's death that he drunk himself to death."

"The others told me that they were brothers as well. They don't look anything alike." Brothers. I supposed that was a good cover story for a pair of assassins. It didn't do them much good. They were both dead now.

"That's what they said," Master Lei shook his head sadly. "I never had any reason to doubt. They were natural performers of exceptional skill. They had such acrobatic talent. How am I going to replace them . . ."

"You found him like this?"

"I was coming around to see if he wanted a drink. I found him like this."

"He obviously had a drink," I said, dryly.

"If I joined him . . . that could have been me," Master Lei

said grimly. He had the look of someone that had just narrowly escaped death. I didn't think he was right. Qiang Ge's tears were dangerous but only deadly to someone that had spent time cultivating their qi—someone like an assassin skilled in qinggong.

Whoever killed the two assassins knew what they were doing. I wondered if the secret of the poison was something that was closely kept and how Old Man Ye knew about it. There was no way to ask him now.

"Do you drink with him often?"

"Quite often. Zhang Yuanhai has been with our troupe for a few years. He keeps to himself, doesn't talk much, but he and I both share a love for Hong's baijiu."

"That stuff tastes disgusting," Jingyi said with a frown.

"I'll admit it's an acquired taste," Master Lei said with a shrug.

"Acquired? More like torture. Brutal, unrelenting torture," she said with a shudder.

"Jingyi," I warned.

"What is it?"

"Hush."

"Sorry."

I turned my attention back to Master Lei. "Tell me about these brothers."

"There's nothing more than I already told you. Zhang Yuanhai had been with us for years but left us for a season. When he came back, he brought his brother with him. That was maybe ten days ago."

"What about the pretty boy, Pian Ren—the kid with the fan?"

"Oh, you mean Dong Jiang. He's been with us for the last three months. I suppose he's new still. Sometimes it feels like you've just known someone forever. That's what it was like with Dong Jiang, like he had been with us for years. The rest of the Cyclone Defenders really like him."

"Is that so? I thought your kind didn't really like newcomers."

"That boy is charming. I mean, did you look at his face? Ever since he came around, the attendance at our shows has tripled. He usually keeps to himself and doesn't socialize too much with the rest of us. He's an odd one out, but I often see him in the company of a new young lady or two."

"I see."

"He said he was a runaway from the Heavenly Mind sect. Never heard of them myself, but I guess they teach some pretty decent *wugong*.[4] He was a natural on stage, and so I paired him up with the other two."

It wasn't unheard of. Funny enough, this wasn't even my first time running into someone that took his martial skills to the stage.

"You didn't notice the obvious tension between them?"

He shrugged. "It's not the first time I've put people that didn't like each other together. Especially when it comes to these sword dances. It adds to the drama. I saw it as a bit of a triumph myself—The three of them on stage together are a big hit. Did you see the show?"

"I saw the show."

He took a deep sigh. "Guess that won't be happening anymore."

"Pretty boy got cut during the performance."

"Oh, that sort of thing happens all the time."

"All the time?" I raised an eyebrow.

"I mean, nothing serious!" Master Lei added quickly. "It's just accidents happen when we perform all the time. The other day, Bu Hao, the fire-breather, caught his clothing on fire!"

Ji Ping made a note and muttered under his breath, "Safety violations . . . need to investigate."

"Did I say accidents happen all the time? I meant nothing happens here. Nothing out of the ordinary at all."

"So what were you really doing coming to his tent?"

"I told you, I was coming here for a drink. Wait, you don't think I'm a suspect here, do you?" He said nervously.

"I don't know. Should I suspect you?"

"No! Absolutely not!" he protested.

"You came here for a drink, and now someone is dead. And now you've had two dead people in your troupe in a single day."

"I'm just trying to do the right thing."

"Which is?"

"Look, I sought him out, thinking he would want a drink. Take his mind off of his brother's death. You know? That kind of thing. Didn't think he'd be dead too," Master Lei shook his head ruefully. "I'm not the bad guy here."

Sometimes, you have to narrow your leads and suspects, but in this case, I already had one. Everything lined up too perfectly. Miao and Pian Ren had motive and opportunity. Afraid for his life? Striking first? Either way, two assassins of the Hidden Fist were dead. Whatever it was, I knew I had to find them.

"Where is Pian Ren?"

"Who?"

I shook my head. *Right, wrong name.* "The pretty boy. Dong Jiang?"

"Oh, young Dong Jiang. I haven't seen him—he always disappears from camp. You think he has something to do with this?"

I ignored him and scooped up the jar of huangjiu, signaling for Ji Ping to coordinate with Mayor Qiao about the body. Without a coroner, I couldn't be sure of anything. But it didn't take a genius to line up the pieces. Pian Ren and Miao were in the middle of this all, with a growing body count.

"We need to find Miao and Pian Ren now," I said.

I could see the shape of the case now. Miao was the obvious culprit. A girl with a background as an assassin, killing assassins? It wasn't much of a logical leap. But there was something else that I needed to confirm first.

"You think they're behind this?" Jingyi frowned.

"I know they are," I said.

"What's with the jar? A little thirsty?" she asked. "You know that's poisoned, right?"

"I'm counting on it."

———

A BLEARY-EYED, SLEEPY, AND GROUCHY YAN TAO OPENED THE door to the inn for us. He seemed tense, annoyed, and a little confused.

"Miao is back," was all he said. Not one for much conversation at this hour of the night, I suppose. He led Jingyi, Ji Ping, Ruo, and I into the main restaurant area without a word.

Miao and the pretty boy sat at a table, a pot of tea with a couple of cups between them. They looked like they had been in intense conversation, and the frown on Miao's face couldn't have been any deeper if a pair of monkeys grabbed the edges of her mouth and yanked. I've seen this kind of conversation plenty of times, been in these too many times to count. A relationship under stress. A lover's quarrel. They looked tired. The young man still wore a bandage around his neck. Miao, for her part, looked stressed. Her hair looked a little wild, and there was a weary kind of alertness in her face that had likely come from watching for unknown threats.

Miao and Pretty Boy looked up when we entered, and they watched as we crossed the room. I sat down at the table across from them, set the jar of huangjiu down in between us, and poured myself a cup of tea. Jingyi and Ji Ping stood at my side, while Ruo leaned against a nearby pillar.

Poison—the subtle touch of murder. The scraps of a plan were coming together. The case made sense. If things went well in the next few minutes, we'd have caught our murderer.

And maybe something more besides.

"Where have you two been?"

"I . . . " Miao started to explain.

"Yan Tao, could we have some fresh tea?" I asked in my nicest voice, cutting her off. Yan Tao's eyes flickered to the teapot on the table but disappeared to the kitchen.

I fixed the pretty boy with a cold stare. "You both owe me an explanation."

"We'll answer your questions, Magistrate," Miao said. And I believed her. I didn't believe her companion's nod, though. "Dong Jiang's real name is Su Da," Miao said, introducing Pian Ren. Ji Ping and Ruo snickered.

"You mean like the famous singer?" I asked.

"Apparently, you're a famous singer too," Pian Ren said, cupping a fist in greeting, but he didn't rise from his seat. *Insolent boy.* "Mister *Jin Min.*"

"It's okay, Miao," I said. I fixed a cold stare at the young man again. He wore the expression of a man coming to the slow realization that his house of lies was about to come tumbling down on top of him, up-turned tile roof and all. And that didn't make him any less handsome. Damn it. "But someone here needs to come clean."

"Come clean?" Miao said, confused. "You said you were going to help us."

"Come clean," I repeated. "There's blood on your hands, and if you don't come clean, it's going to stain."

"It's okay, Miao. We'll be able to be together soon enough," Pian Ren said, putting a hand soothingly on her arm.

She nodded, her eyes beaming. "Just be patient, Su Da. I'll get you somewhere safe."

"I know, Miao. You're the only one I feel safe with."

I tried not to gag.

Miao didn't see it. But everyone else saw it. Jingyi flinched. Ji Ping rolled his eyes. Even Ruo looked like he was about to vomit. But not Miao. At least knowing what I knew, I could see right through it. But at the same time, damn, this kid was good. I suppose I shouldn't be so hard on the young woman. What did she know? She just barely escaped from an assassin clan and was still trying to discover her own place in the world. Of course, when a handsome face came along and told her she was beautiful and the only one that could help him, she'd be powerless.

I made up my mind then. We would have to do what we could to save Miao.

"I'll give you one more chance," I said. I reached for the teacups and began pouring the huangjiu into three cups and slid two of them to Miao and Pian Ren. "But first, why don't you two join me? Please drink."

Yan Tao brought over fresh tea to the table, looked at the jar of huangjiu, and then grumbled something about wasting his time with tea if we were just going to drink wine.

Miao reached for her cup, pausing only for a moment at the strangeness of my request. Pian Ren didn't reach for his at all. I cradled my cup, swirled the contents around.

"Tell him what's going on, Su Da," Miao urged, touching Pian Ren on his arm. "Mister Jin Min is actually a magistrate. He can help us."

"Don't worry, Miao. Whatever happens, we'll face it together."

Us? Oh, no.

"You'll face it together. How cute," I scowled. "Well I'll have you know that 'together' you're both in a lot of trouble."

"I know," Miao said, nodding her head soberly. "Su Da is on the run from the Hidden Fist."

"I don't know why they're after me! You have to help me, Magistrate," the young man said with some desperation.

"Tell me about yourself, Su Da," I asked.

"Is this really the time and place for it?"

"Yes."

He sighed and then began telling a tragic tale of how his parents died when he was young and misfortune befell his family at every turn. Something about plague and famine, and then fire and adventure, and other stuff that I didn't really pay attention to. To tell the truth, I stopped listening after I asked him about himself. It really didn't matter. I held up a hand to cut him off.

"Enough of that."

"Mister Jin Min?"

"Blah, blah, blah. Boring. I have a better idea. Let's drink." I raised my cup to toast them. "To your longevity and good health."

Miao raised the cup and repeated my toast. The moment seemed to drag out forever as I watched to see if she would drink, to see if she would detect the poison in it. The cup touched her lips.

Pian Ren batted it out of her hand. "No!"

The cup spilled its contents on the table, and Miao turned to Pian Ren in confusion and anger. "What?"

"What the hell are you doing, boy?" Yan Tao growled.

"Why did you do that?" she asked.

"Yes, why did you do that?" I asked Pian Ren.

"I . . . uhm . . . she shouldn't be drinking."

"Why not?"

"Well, liquor isn't good for you . . ." Pian Ren said, hurriedly. "You shouldn't drink."

"He's got a point, but that's not it. This huangjiu is poisoned."

"You saved my life, Su Da!" Miao gasped, but then a look of confusion settled on her face. "But I don't understand, Mister Jin Min. Why are you trying to poison me?"

"I'm not trying to poison you," I shook my head. "But before we get into that, let's drop all pretenses, shall we? Su Da isn't your real name."

"Of course, it's my real name," the pretty boy said.

"You're mistaken . . ." Miao started.

"I'm afraid I'm not, Miao," I sighed. "While we're at it, my name isn't Jin Min either. It's Tao Jun. I am Magistrate Tao Jun."

I let it sink in for a moment, and then Miao's eyes widened. "You're Magistrate Tao Jun, the governor's special investigator!" She stammered. "The magistrate of the torch!"

"That's exactly right," I chuckled and poured myself a cup of the tea Yan Tao brought and took a sip. "What a lovely blend, Yan Tao. This is the best tea I've ever had."

"Liar," Yan Tao mumbled. "It's the cheapest one I have."

I ignored him.

"Now, I want to help, but there's something I don't understand here. I've got three dead people on my hands, and somehow you two are both at the center of it all." I gave them both a dark glare. Miao shivered under my gaze. Pian Ren didn't flinch. "I've got Huang Lian, someone that was supposed to help you, murdered in An'lin. Then I've got two acrobats—the Zhang brothers—dead in a single day, both without any traces of foul play."

"Those two were assassins from the Hidden Fist," Miao said firmly.

"I only have your word that they were, Miao," I said, shaking my head. "There's no proof they were from the Hidden Fist."

"But . . ."

"You'll forgive me if I don't feel sorry for their deaths," the pretty boy tugged down the bandage around his neck and pointed at the thin red line there. "They were going to kill me and make it into a performance accident."

"I thought you said they wanted to bring you in alive."

"That too," he said quickly.

"I'm going to be honest with you both. Whatever situation you were in before, this has turned into a murder investigation. And you two are my prime suspects. Do you have any idea how much trouble you're in?"

That shut up the pretty boy.

"I'm sure you've never had to consider what kind of punishments the law can bring to bear. After all, this is the *jianghu*. So many affairs are settled outside the periphery of the law," I set my cup down. "But I've been dragged into this. And now you can't escape it."

Miao looked ready to stammer something, but I didn't give her space to speak.

"Here's what's in store for a triple murder. Prison is certainly a possibility. But what are we really looking at here, Ji Ping?"

"Beheading," Ji Ping said, matter-of-factly.

"Beheading," I repeated with relish.

Miao looked stricken. Pian Ren just glowered.

"But, Magistrate," Miao said, "how did they die? I didn't see any puncture wounds or anything on the assassin when I was with you."

"That's the genius of it, isn't it? You tell me, Miao. How did you do it? How did you kill both of them? Though I'm sure someone of your skills would be able to kill people in a wide variety of ways."

"What is this?" Su Da said, interrupting. "How dare you talk to her like that?"

I slammed my hand down on the table, startling everyone. Yan Tao and Ji Ping cursed, and Jingyi and Ruo tensed. "Be silent, boy." I pulled out my seal and set it on the table between us. "That little seal. That gives me the authority to talk to anyone however I want. You seem to think you know what's going. Tell me, what's happening?"

"An interrogation."

"Give the man a prize!" I said, clapping. "You're a smart one."

His eyes narrowed. "I thought you had to do interrogations at the tribunal. That was the law."

"For someone that bends the law so much, you seem to know a lot about it."

"I like to know my rights."

"I'm sure," I nodded. I leaned in, letting out a deep sigh. "Miao, Su Da is lying to you," I said without taking my stare off of Pian Ren.

"Like you're one to talk, Magistrate. You haven't said a single thing that's true this whole time!" he said, shaking his head. He looked to Miao for support. "Miao, my name is Su Da. You know I'm telling the truth. You have to believe me."

She nodded.

"Miao, this man is a con man."

"No," she said flatly.

"No?" I asked.

"No," she insisted.

"Ji Ping?"

"Yes, Excellency?" Ji Ping came froward, giving me a slight bow.

"Tell me the story of Pian Ren."

"Pian Ren—who goes by many aliases—is wanted for the robbery of the Wu family in Tu'men and the defrauding of three government officials. He is also wanted in connection to the murder of two government officials in He'bian and for the destruction of a fireworks workshop in Tu'men and the death of fifty people," he said, pulling a bulletin out of his sleeve. "I'm lucky the local clerk had a copy of this."

He had the audacity to laugh. "You think this guy is me?"

"Yes," I said simply.

Ji Ping placed a sketch of the primary suspect on the table for all to see. Apart from the hair looking longer and a few details around the mouth, it looked just like the pretty boy.

"This is outrageous! We came here for help from you, and now you're throwing these accusations at me? We don't have to take this, Miao. Let's go," he started to rise.

Ruo was there in a moment with a heavy hand on his shoulder. "Please sit, young man. The magistrate isn't done with you yet," his deep voice rumbled through the room. Pian Ren turned to look up at the big man and then blanched. The chair creaked as he sat down.

"You kill anyone that comes close to you or figuring it out!" I was shouting at this point. I didn't care who I woke up. "You killed Zhang Yuanjun and Zhang Yuanhai with Qiang Ge's Tears!"

"It wasn't me!"

"Then why did you stop Miao from drinking the wine?" I yelled. He glared in response but kept his mouth shut. "I'll tell you why. Because you recognized this jar. This is the jar that you gave to Zhang Yuanhai to drink. This is the jar that killed him. This is the jar that you poisoned!"

He made to stand up, but Ruo now had both hands on his shoulders, pushing the young man firmly back into the seat.

I placed my sword on the table, in a not so subtle signal.

"We can do this the hard way if you really want. You may think your *wugong* is strong enough to take on someone like me. But I'll have you know that I'm a swordsman of Blue Mountain."

Here's another tip, and I don't like to admit to this one, but sometimes you have to convince[1] people to work with you. And sometimes you have to be a little more forceful in convincing them. I pushed out with my qi, using it to smother Pian Ren. He had some training, and I felt a bit of resistance, but I was far stronger, and there was no way he could resist. I was going to push even further and break him under the force of my qi when I felt a hand on my shoulder. Jingyi shook her head.

"Not like this," Jingyi said.

I let the kid go, and he panicked.

"You don't actually think that's me, do you, Miao?"

Miao had gone pale. She couldn't take her eyes off of the picture.

"Miao has tried really hard to protect you. She found Huang Lian to help you, and now he's dead," Jingyi added.

"She found me to help you, and you almost let her drink poison. But that's out of character for you. You were going to kill Miao, too, once you were free and clear, weren't you? How many more dead are you going to leave in your wake?"

"I didn't have anything to do with it!" he said, rising and backing away from the table. He pointed at the girl. "It was Miao! She's a—"

Jingyi grabbed Pian Ren by the hand and twisted. He squirmed and crumpled under her grip. Miao's hand shook, whether from anger or a shock, I couldn't tell.

"I apologize, Miao. I wouldn't have really poisoned you. Qiang Ge's tears are practically undetectable, unless you've been exposed to it before. It was a ploy to draw out Pian Ren," I was trying not to expose Miao's secret past. I was also trying to avoid Yan Tao's glare. I'd have to make it up to him somehow.

"You used me?" Miao said, her voice trembling.

"Pian Ren used you," I shrugged. "I saved you."

"Magistrate . . ." Ji Ping said.

"As for the rest, I have it figured out. Pian Ren, you worked with the Zhang brothers to pull off the attack on the imperial treasury convoy. While they dealt with the main convoy, your job was to poison the decoys. You learned from your allies that the decoy convoys were led by treasury guards that had martial training, so you used Qiang Ge's Tears to take care of them . . . disrupting their flow of qi. But somewhere along the line, you double crossed your allies, didn't you? Did you want a bigger cut for yourself? Needed to pay for some mistress somewhere?"

Miao blushed.

"You were the one that destroyed the fireworks factory in Tu'men. At first, I didn't get how that could be related to the attack on the treasury convoy, but then it made sense. What a stage for a perfect con. They wanted you dead, so you lured them there to kill them first."

"By destroying the factory?" asked Jingyi.

"Fifty people dead, just to cover his tracks," Ji Ping scowled.

I could feel Yan Tao's glare still, though it seemed to alternate between me and the pretty boy.

"That was a nice touch! Destroying the factory and killing all those people. It should have worked. But what went wrong? You already planned for your survival, but you obviously didn't plan for theirs. You made a mistake."

"I don't make mistakes."

"Your whole life is a mistake!" I laughed. Miao flinched, and Pian Ren seethed. "One after another—a life on the run. You run from all the mistakes of your life. But you thought you finally got away with it, didn't you? You hid with a performance troupe, thinking it was a good place to lie low since they travelled. But again, another mistake!" I roared with laughter. "You joined the wrong group! Your old friends with the Hidden Fist found you, and you panicked. But by this time, you made friends with Miao, the perfect fall girl. She liked you right from the start, and she tried to help you by bringing in Righteous Will's Huang Lian. A good man that happened to be trying to help the wrong person.

"The Zhang brothers found you in the Cyclone Defenders' troupe, and Miao warned you that they were assassins. But you already knew this, didn't you? So you started formulating a plan, a way to kill them both before they got to you."

"They were going to kill me! What else was I supposed to do? They were going to kidnap me and take me back to their leaders," he shuddered. "That's a fate worse than death. If you had Hidden Fist assassins after you, you'd do the same."

And there it was. That was all I needed.[2]

"Maybe. Maybe not."

The pretty boy slumped at the table, burying his face in his hands. His body trembled, and at first I thought he was crying. Then I heard the laughter.

"They were so stupid. I told them I would come willingly with them, and we shared a drink in agreement. I didn't even have to force it on them."

"And with them dead, if anyone suspected you, you could easily point to Miao and her checkered past as a suspect. But that was before our arrival forced you to change your plan."

"You used me?" Miao asked again, turning to Pian Ren. There was hurt in her voice and confusion and something else I knew too well. I braced myself. Here it came.

"I . . ."

Miao abruptly stood up and punched Pian Ren hard. He fell to the ground, groaning. Ji Ping and Yan Tao winced. I nodded with approval.

"You're lucky she didn't put her real strength into that. You'd be dead."

"Is all of his true?" she asked angrily. Pian Ren had the wisdom to keep his mouth shut.

From somewhere behind me I heard Yan Tao mutter, "See, I told you the girl could take care of herself."

"Things changed, Miao. I couldn't see you hurt yourself."

"I don't believe you," Miao said. The hurt in her voice made me cringe. Look, I'm not completely heartless okay? I don't *like* to ruin people's lives.

"It's true, Miao. I love you!"

We all groaned. Even Yan Tao rolled his eyes.

"Okay, lover boy. That's enough." Ruo hefted the guy back up to his feet. "Now, what do we do? Haul him back to An'lin?"

"I suppose that's what we need to do," Ji Ping said. "Mister Yan Tao, do you have any rope?"

"Magistrate, may I say something?" Miao said quietly.

"Please," I nodded at her.

"Magistrate, by killing those two, he's likely brought down the Hidden Fist on us all. "

"When do you think they'll be here?"

"They may already be here."

I cursed. "What do you think they'll do?"

"Well, they'll probably tear the whole place apart looking for him."

"For not wanting to drag Yan Tao into this, you sure picked a bad way to show it," I said angrily. Teenagers. "We need to get ready."

"Miao, you and Yan Tao need to get somewhere safe. You have other guests here. Protect them."

"I'm joining you."

"Miao, you can't stay. You need to look after Yan Tao and the other guests. Besides," I said quietly. "The Hidden Fist can't know that you're involved."

"But . . ."

"You'll be helping me out more by staying safe, Miao. Please."

She gave me a single nod.

"What are you planning?" Jingyi asked.

"I have an idea, and you're going to help."

"Oh good."

8

————————

"MAGISTRATE TAO JUN! PLEASE HELP. YOU'RE THE ONLY ONE that can fix it!"

Can't they find someone else to do it?

"But that's your job, Magistrate!" they'll say.

And so I have to do it. Sometimes that means I go grab my sword, summon a squad of guards, and we go break something. Sometimes it means I go have a 'pleasant' conversation with someone, threaten imperial wrath, break some pots and furniture, and go along on my merry way.

I've been called a thug. I've been called a bully.

Those are the good days of bad cases.

The bad days? Escorting dignitaries around. Bowing and scraping to make sure I don't accidentally offend someone that probably deserved it. Hours of meetings. Days spent pouring over documents. Even with adjutants and assistants, I still have to look over papers and stamp and seal more things than I like.

Look, it's not that I don't like my job, it has its perks. It's just sometimes I wish that people could solve their own problems, you know? Maybe they could have a reasonable conversation with another person without drawing weapons.

Then maybe I don't have to go look at another corpse and piece together what happened, figure out who to arrest and who to execute.

Of course, it takes someone with a level head to sort out these problems. Which is, I suppose, why people come to me with their problems. They think I'm the one that can have a conversation for them so they don't have to. I'm a magistrate, so I have a level head.

They couldn't be more wrong.

Still, that's how I ended up with a sword in hand waiting for a bunch of assassins outside of an inn that specializes in broken furniture, Jingyi beside me. Above us, colorful lanterns hung from the eaves. A bright counterpoint to the orange glow from the stone lanterns of the walkway. The night was still, no wind. But there was a heaviness in the air, a chill that seemed on the edge of frost. Or maybe it was just in my head.

I wasn't sure where tonight ranked on my range of good and bad cases, but I was pretty sure waiting for assassins didn't count as good. My people were inside, though Officer Ruo waited with Pian Ren on the other side of the door. I had something special planned for them. Miao was with Yan Tao, Ji Ping, and the other guests. Hopefully, somewhere safe and not doing anything stupid.

"This is partially your fault," I told Miao.

"I'm sorry, Magistrate," she had said.

Even one-armed, I figured she would make a good last line of defense. Look, you might think I was being hard on the girl, and maybe I shouldn't have made her stand guard. You're right. I was hard on her. I hope she learns something from this mess and never ends up getting conned by a pretty face again. I don't like punishing people for being trusting and a little bit naive. She had a good heart. There's nothing wrong with that. And I hate it when good people end up in bad situations because of the dishonest. Here's the thing: I don't care too much about the law or mountains of bureaucracy. What I do care about is the wrong people getting hurt. And this was a situation where a lot of the wrong people were going to get hurt. Justice, the law, all of that is supposed to protect the wrong people from getting hurt. And if the imperial bureaucracy didn't like how I went about ensuring justice, then they can fire me. But even without a magistrate's seal, I wouldn't stop.

That's not how it works.

Jingyi stretched beside me. "Tell me again why I'm helping to save the life of the guy that is responsible for my man's death?"

"Because if you don't help me out, a lot of people innocent people are going to get caught in the middle of this."

"Ugh," she complained. "You're really the worst. I knew coming to you for help was a bad idea."

That one hurt a little, given where we were now. "My apologies, Mistress Bai. But I had no way of knowing that when you came into my office, an assassin clan would be waiting at the end of this."

She grumbled something under her breath that I couldn't understand. Probably for the best.

It didn't take long for the Hidden Fist to show up. If there's something you should know about assassins, it's this: they like drama. Sometimes they do that shadowy trick where they just melt out of the darkness and appear before you. Or sometimes they throw down a smoke bomb, and while everyone is busy coughing and wheezing, they drop ropes and materialize and begin their dark deeds. In short, assassins live up to their reputations for being mysterious and frightening.

They did not do any of that tonight. And here's the other thing you should know about assassins: sometimes they act like normal people. In fact, the best assassins I knew had normal jobs and normal lives and did nothing suspicious. It wasn't until they acted that we realized who and what they actually were. Scary stuff. This bunch rode up the road on horseback—ten of them—and dismounted in front of the inn.

Not really the kind of arrival I was expecting, but one that made sense. They were dressed like ordinary people, some in the garb of merchants, some in the clothes of farmers and villagers. Perfectly ordinary, and no doubt spies and informants planted in all levels of society. Well, they were ordinary except for the masks made of black cloth, but even that's fairly ordinary for bandits and their like. Still, they brought the numbers to the party, and it was clear they weren't going to mess around.

Five of them approached, and one hung back. Three brought bows to bear and lit torches for fire arrows. I cursed to myself. A play right out of my own book.

"Good evening, friends, and welcome to the Green Brocade Inn," I said, striding forward. "Unfortunately, we're closed right now. If you come back in the morning, we'll be happy to host you."

They didn't answer and instead brandished weapons. Swords for the most part, it looked like. I could handle swords. No problem. I am a swordsman, after all. It was the archers in the back that I was worried about. I wasn't sure what kind of fuel combination the Hidden Fist had brought with them, but I was sure they weren't messing around.

"Can you handle arrow deflection?" I whispered to Jingyi. "They could burn down the whole place with a handful of those fire arrows. I can handle the guys on the ground."

"I'll deal with it," she said and with a *qinggong*-assisted leap and a kick off the restaurant's two main pillars, she was up onto the roof.

Bows creaked as they were drawn into position.

"Hold on! There's no need for this to turn violent," I shouted. "I'm sure we can come to an understanding."

No response. I have to hand it to them—assassins don't

talk much. They are people of action. When they're going to go, they're going to go. They're not like bandits. You can interrupt those guys and throw them off with a little banter and taunting. Assassins? Well, a good one is strictly professional. All business.

At a signal from the one in the back, they began their attack. Arrows launched in orange streaks of light. Jingyi was true to her word. Each arrow was met by a sweep of her spear, clattering down to the ground below. She spun and twisted, whipping her weapon around in a defensive pattern. In the flickering light of the arrows and lanterns, she looked every part the martial hero of storytelling legend.

It was no wonder she had a fan club. If Officer Ruo was peeking through the windows, I was sure he was swooning. I had no time to watch. Three launched themselves at me, while two leaped up onto the roof.

In a silver blur, I unsheathed Joy and swept my blade around to meet their swords. I drew them into my tempo, a steady rhythm of attacks, feints, and parries. When the moment was right, I channeled my qi for the Sword of the Nine Dragon's signature attack—*Echo of the Blue Mountain.*

It's hard to describe the thrill I get when I do this. I know as a magistrate I'm not really supposed to get excited about fighting. A fight usually means I've failed at my job. But I like to look at it as not a failure but as an opportunity to teach a lesson. Aggressive negotiations—if you will. Am I a bad guy if I love the way the warm tingle of qi spread through my body, the singing of the blood in my veins, the rush of adrenaline? No, I'm not.

Joy shivered as my qi poured into it, and it passed easily through each of the three swords, shattering them as it met each blade. To their credit, the assassins weren't too surprised and quickly tried to switch to the daggers they carried (you can always count on an assassin to bring more than one weapon to the party), but my follow up strikes found one in the throat and took another's hand.

The third retreated and began circling, searching for an opening. Someone fell from the roof, and out of the corner of my eye I saw that it was one of Jingyi's attackers.

"Wait, wait, wait!" I called out as the third settled into a fighting stance again. The archers had stopped their volleys and were readying weapons to join the fray. "No one else has to die here today."

"It's a little too late for that," Jingyi called out, burying her spear into the other rooftop attacker and riding him to the ground. I ignored her.

"You're here to avenge the death of your brothers, I get that," I said, lowering my sword. "But you have to understand that Green Brocade had nothing to do with it."

"Green Brocade is sheltering the one who killed them!" called out the one in the back.

"Are you the leader of this bunch? If you're the leader, why don't you come over here so we can chat." When the man in the back didn't move, I added, "I have something you want."

"You have nothing we want."

"Are you so sure?" I asked. "Officer Ruo! Bring your package out here, please."

The door of the inn slid open, and the burly frame of Officer Ruo stepped out, carrying Pian Ren on his shoulder. The con man was tied up and had a burlap sack over his head. Ruo came to my side, then dropped the pretty boy on the ground unceremoniously in front of me. Pian Ren let out a groan.

"This is Dong Jiang."

"Who is that?"

"Oh? How about Pian Ren?"

A head shake.

"How about Su Da?"

Another head shake. I had a moment of mild panic. Was this really the wrong guy? I took a quick breath, remembering that even if I was wrong, there were lives at stake.

"That could be anyone. It could even be that fat innkeeper that runs the place."

"How could this be the fat innkeeper?" I let out an exasperated groan. "He's not even fat." Seeing that they weren't convinced, I yanked the sack off of the con man's head, then gestured for Ruo to bring over a torch to show the man's face. "The point is, this is the guy that's responsible for the deaths of your brothers. He's the one that double crossed you during the treasury raid."

"Pu Yao! Did you think you could get away?" the leader hissed. "You really thought you could steal from us?"

"Geez, how many aliases does this guy have?" Jingyi muttered.

"He's who you're looking for, right? Well, you can have him . . . for a price." I said.

"You're in no position to negotiate," their leader called out.

"I'm in every position to negotiate. We just killed four of your little hit squad, and we didn't even try yet."

"What's to stop us from just killing you and taking our prize?"

"You have no idea who I am, do you?"

They shrugged.

"I'm not some Jianghu wannabe. I'm Magistrate Tao Jun of An'lin."

"Likely story."

"You don't look like a magistrate."

"I'm in disguise," I said, pulling the magistrate seal from my sash. I held it up for them to see. I doubted they could make out any details in the dim lantern light, but held it firm in my hand. I've done this part a thousand times. It wasn't the seal that sold it. It was the confidence, the swagger.

And I'm all swagger.

"I am Magistrate Tao Jun. I could arrest you all right now."

"You try, and we'll kill you."

I laughed. "Is that all you assassins are good for? Killing? Listen to reason. You kill me and every guard in An'lin will come after you and wipe you and your little sect out."

"A bluff."

I shrugged. "Maybe. But you can find out the hard way. I have sent orders back to An'lin to exterminate all the Hidden Fist they find if something were to happen to me[1]. Back at the tribunal, we have quite the file on your activities. We know exactly what you do, exactly where you've hidden yourselves. We know about your people in the governor's palace. We know about your people in the markets." I paused, letting the tension build up between us[2]. "And we already know that you're the ones responsible for the attack on the treasury convoy. You worked with a con man to steal the emperor's gold. You kill me and you bring down the imperial tribunal down on you in every city in the kingdom."

They were quiet for a while. I gripped Joy in my hand, waiting for the moment to break. There was no file. There was no backup. This was all bluff.

"You lie!" one of the assassins yelled out. I guess he got tired of waiting. He lunged, and I spun to dodge the attack. Jingyi was there before me and beat him over the head with her spear. He crumpled to the ground, and she stood on his back with her spear aimed at his neck.

"Like I said, we'll wipe you all out right now if that's what you want. But that's not what I want."

The leader whistled, and the assassins sheathed their weapons and returned to his side.

"You'll give him to us?"

"Yes, and you don't trouble the inn anymore."

"What?" Jingyi gaped. "You're giving him to them?"

I shushed her.

"What do you get out of this?" the leader asked.

"I want to meet your boss. Send them to me in the capital."

"I'll pass along the message," he said after a moment's consideration. "We'll see what they decide."

"Hold on. How do I know that you'll keep your word?" I've had enough experience with goons to know I needed proof.

The leader approached and handed me a carved jade token. I couldn't make out the details in this light, but it felt like it was intricately carved.

"This is my token."

"How do I know this isn't just some piece of stone you had in your pocket?"

The assassin glared at me. "It's the token of a squad leader. Present it to the right people. Tell them Bird sent you."

I nodded. Of course, I had no idea who the 'right people' were, but that was a problem for another time. I took a step backward and gestured for the assassins to take Pian Ren away.

"You can't do this to me! They're going to kill me!" Pian Ren protested through his gag.

"We were going to kill you anyway. You would have been executed in An'lin in front of the governor. You had no escape from imperial law. This just solved two problems at once.[3] And who knows, the Hidden Fist might show you some mercy."

They tied him to the back of one of the horses. The leader signaled for the others to collect their dead, and without another word, they rode away.

"Maybe." I said to myself.

"What just happened?" Ji Ping said as their retreating figures disappeared into the night. By now, he, Miao, and Yan Tao had emerged from the inn. Officer Ruo shrugged and began giving furtive glances to Jingyi, hoping she would notice him and talk to him.

"You can do this?" Jingyi asked. She didn't notice Officer Ruo. "Won't you get in trouble for this?"

Officer Ruo laughed. It was an ugly sound. "Magistrate Tao Jun doesn't get into trouble. He's the governor's favorite."

I shrugged. "I make the decisions that the governor turns a blind eye to so he doesn't have to make them. Besides, it doesn't hurt to have a group like the Hidden Fist in your debt."

Jingyi didn't look like she believed me, but I didn't care. "Is this how justice is supposed to work around here?"

"Imperial justice doesn't always work. More often than not, it hurts the people that it's supposed to protect." I shook my head. "If we took Pian Ren, then the Hidden Fist would have burned this place to the ground. That wouldn't have been the right solution. Correct?"

Jingyi hesitated, then gave a single nod. It wasn't the best answer, but it would have to do.

"Sometimes the only good choice is the one between bad and worse." I gave her a wry grin. "Besides, if the governor doesn't like it, he can fire me. I don't mind."

9

"IF ONLY YOU'D FIGURED OUT WHERE THE GOLD WENT, THEN THIS would be a big win," Captain Chen said. "And I'm surprised the governor isn't furious with you. You don't really have anything to show for all that work."

I shrugged, tipping my futou back for a nap.

"You can't take a nap here! This is a magistrate's office," Ji Ping chided.

"It's my office, and I can do what I want, Ji Ping," I stuck my tongue out at him.

"Seems like the money is the only thing the governor cares about," Captain Chen observed. "He didn't even care that much about what happened to Pian Ren."

"Like I told him, the money is probably long gone. It's been over three months. The Hidden Fist and their allies have probably already spent it." I said. "Besides, he's stressed out about the Black Tiger rebellion."

Captain Chen was wrong there. The governor certainly cared what happened to Pian Ren, but he didn't want to make a big deal out of it. Huang Lian's murder had become the talk of the town, and a murder in one of the finer restaurants in town demanded answers. When we returned to An'lin, I wrote my report, and I discussed it with the governor in private.

He frowned the entire time but applauded my quick thinking in resolving the crisis to an "acceptable" conclusion. We discussed the details of the case, and he decided that pinning it on the Hidden Fist would be tactless.

"It would upset some people," he said, and we left it at that.

In short, I was expected to sweep all of this under the rug. It wasn't the first time I realized it, but it was fairly obvious this time. The governor was on someone else's payroll—He didn't care about justice.

Jingyi didn't like it. She made her displeasure very clear to me when she came storming into my office earlier in the day. But she didn't have a say in the matter either.

"I can't believe this. Huang Lian got killed trying to figure out what happened with your missing treasury convoy. Where's the justice?" she had said.

"Justice?" This again. She wouldn't let up. "How much justice are you expecting? The Hidden Fist assassin, Zhang Yuanjun, was responsible for killing Huang Lian. And then Pian Ren killed him."

"So I should be thanking Pian Ren?"

"Whatever you want. That's up to you."

"You just handed him over to the Hidden Fist without consulting any of us."

"Miss Bai, do you really expect me to consult with you? You forget yourself. I'm the magistrate here."

"But there's no public trial . . ."

"Does it matter if it was under our hand or someone else?"

"And the truth . . ."

"The truth doesn't matter, Jingyi. You and I know that he died as a good man."

"I don't like how you do things, Magistrate," she said, annoyed.

"I know," I said, shaking my head. "But at least the censorate aren't digging into this. Huang Lian is likely at peace now."

"Thank you for your help," she bowed, then turned to leave. I couldn't tell if she was being sincere. She was obviously upset that things didn't go the way she wanted.

Then again, what in life ever goes the way we want?

"Wait," I said, letting out a sigh. She stopped, turned her head to look at me over her shoulder. I pulled out a scroll from my desk. "This is for you."

"What is it?"

"A gift. A commendation from the governor for your fine service in this case, stamped with his seal. I thought you'd want something to take back to the censorate. That should help you clear some of the heat on your company."

For a moment I thought Jingyi was getting all misty-eyed and was going to cry, but she just bowed again. "Thank you, magistrate. That's most kind."

"I know, I know."

She wanted the truth? Truth was, there were days I didn't like how I did things either. I weave a web of half-truths and lies in the pursuit of justice because sometimes imperial law punishes the wrong people. Sometimes it lets people through the gaps that have no business being free. And sometimes it just ruins everyone's lives.

The system works, sure. But when you need anything really done, then it all comes down to who you know and what kind of favors they owe you. A little greased palm here and there. An envelope of promissory notes. A silver ingot in the right place.

That's how the system really works. That was the truth that ruled our lives from my informant Lai Wu and his cart of shady and illegally obtained merchandise to the governor on his throne. We all owed someone and someone owed us. The only one that got any real justice was the emperor on his distant throne, and even then, he was bound. We're all trapped with our little roles we play, so what if I broke the rules a little to make sure someone out there got a scrap of happiness?

"We'll likely have to put our efforts into rooting out the rebellion in An'lin soon," Ji Ping said, breaking me from my recollection. Was that a note of regret? It sounded like a note of regret. "The Black Tigers are everywhere."

"No more shows for us," Officer Ruo added sadly. "I don't think the Cyclone Defenders are going to be performing for a while."

"Do you think the Hidden Fist is helping to fund the Black Tiger Rebellion?" Captain Chen mused.

"No idea," Ji Ping said. "I wasn't aware of any connection between the two."

"Well, the Black Tigers have been hiring groups out of the *jianghu* so . . ."

"No sense in speculating too much," I said, cutting off further speculation. Speculation between those two led to heated debates, which lead to shouting, and then no one gets a nap.

There was a knock on the door, and a tribunal clerk slid it open to make way for a beautiful noblewoman. She entered my office with a smile and a nod to the young clerk, who blushed and scurried away. She was older than me, but she was definitely a head turner. Even Ji Ping stopped talking when she entered.

It's not often that I find a beautiful woman that I don't know in my office. But this one was different. She sat with the regal posture of a queen and walked with the confidence of an underworld crime lord. And even though she smiled, she did it with a sense of superiority, an imperious gaze that gave me shivers.

She reminded me of Lady Yue[1] of An'lin. I'm always on the wrong side of her glares, too, and it's never pleasant.

"Magistrate Tao Jun?" she asked. At least her tone was pleasant. It had a warmth that was at once charming, alluring.

This lady was dangerous.

"Yes?" I asked, straightening up.

"You sent for me?"

I'm sure I looked like an idiot as I tried to figure out what she was talking about.

"You sent a message to some of my associates. A bird invited me to pay you a visit."

Bird?

"That's right." I rose from my seat and bowed to her in greeting. "Gentlemen, please excuse us."

Captain Chen and Ji Ping gave the woman a doubtful look as they filed past, while Officer Ruo gave me a wink. I scowled and hurried them all out.

"What can I do for you . . . Lady?"

"You can call me Lady Shu."

"Lady Shu," I smiled my most charming smile and offered her seat. "What can I do for you?"

"I'm here to thank you for returning what is rightfully mine. Pu Yao's return kept certain people safe."

Pu Yao? Right, another alias of Pian Ren.

"Kind of sloppy, isn't it? Letting a con man steal your secrets."

"You know how it is," she sighed. "Good help is hard to find."

In a strange sort of way, I totally understood.

"Such a tragedy. If that young man hadn't thought to betray us, then there would have been no need for this," she fixed me with a curious smile. "Still, I have to give him credit. Qiang Ge's Tears was an inspired and subtle touch. I didn't expect it from him."

"He almost got away with it too," I shook my head. "I want to understand what happened."

"I can't tell you much. You aren't a client."

"Tell me what you can then."

"One of our squads was working with him on a job. But then he stole some of our sect's secrets."

"Sounds juicy."

"Of the juiciest kind," she said with a flirtatious wink.

"Seems like he took something of yours as well as ours."

"A pity."

"Where is the gold, Lady Shu?"

"You have my gratitude for Pu Yao. But not that much of my gratitude."

"Uh-huh."

She rose and walked to the window. Even though it was overcast, the light of the day lit up her fine features. There was a delicateness there, one that seemed to flit in and out of her expressions like a mask. "So, you asked me to come and see you. Here I am. What do you want?"

"I gave you what you wanted. But I want some reassurances."

"Go ahead," she said without turning away from the window.

"I don't really care what happened to the gold. That's between you and your clients."

"How kind of you."

I shrugged. "That's not really my problem."

"And you don't get involved in other people's problems?"

She had me there. "Oh, I get involved all the time. But you see, there has to be something in it for me."

"And what is it you want?"

"You leave the Green Brocade Inn alone. No reprisals. And you leave Miao unharmed."

"Miao?"

"Don't play dumb. You know who I mean. It was no coincidence her former clan came sniffing around her."

"There's no fooling you, is there?" Lady Shu said with that pleasant smile again. "That girl doesn't know it, but she started something big in the Hidden Fist."

"You let her go, didn't you?"

She nodded. "Change is good for our organization. We've been stuck in the old ways too long. Every once in a while we need to clean house."

"I see," I said, nodding. "So, you're cleaning house now? Last I checked, whenever assassins did housecleaning, they leave bodies behind. From what I understand, cleaners don't leave a trail of blood."

"You're cute."

"What's to stop me from arresting you?"

"You're not going to do that."

"I'm a magistrate. That's my job."

"But how often do you *really* do your job, Magistrate Tao Jun?" she said, her voice a purring in my ear. "Your reputation precedes you. You like to play fast and loose with the law, Mister Magistrate of the Torch. The Hidden Fist just deals with loose ends, and you and I both know that the fabric of society is cut and sewn by people like us. We all have to be a little flexible to get things done."

"You've got a point there," I said, shrugging.

"So, you asked for my presence, and here I am. What am I doing here, Magistrate? Something you need to do without getting your hands dirty?"

"Oh, I'm perfectly willing to get my hands dirty," I chuckled. "It's my robes I don't like to get dirty."

"Then what do *you* propose," she turned from the window, a shadow on half her face, her voice that dark purr, "Magistrate Tao Jun?"

And there it was. Another favor to add to my collection.

"I think we can help each other out." I gave her a smile. She returned it. "I'm sure."

MAGISTRATE TAO JUN'S STORY WILL CONTINUE.

THE TALE OF THE MAGISTRATE PT. 2

THE HAND OF REVENGE

Magistrate Tao Jun is bored.

How could he not be? Life in An'lin is quiet—a little too quiet.

So when a series of murders, disturbs the peace, Magistrate Tao Jun is on the case. But when one dead body leads to another dead body and another, a disturbing ghost from the magistrate's past will rear its ugly head. Suddenly caught in a race against time against a deadly serial killer, Tao Jun will face his toughest challenge yet.

Out in 2022.

NOTES

Chapter 1

1. The clerk was fine. Everyone was fine. Heck, even the crazy man was fine. And it was only five drops on the hem—far from the disaster Magistrate Tao Jun makes it out to be.
2. A black hat with two oval-shaped wings to the side. Almost like Mickey Mouse ears before Mickey was cool.
3. Martial arts.
4. A *youtiao* is a type of fried bread that is stretched out. Kind of like a donut.
5. *Jielan*, also known as kailan is a type of broccoli. Very tasty.
6. *Cough* His father pulled some strings to get him promoted. Much to his naysayers' chagrin, it turned out that Tao Jun is actually good at his job and has since been promoted on his own merit.
7. Not the most subtle of men, Magistrate Tao Jun burned a whole village down. The bandits disbanded shortly after. While excessive, the bandits were a plague on the trade routes, and there was much rejoicing when they disbanded.
8. Not probably. Definitely.
9. *Xiaojie* means miss and is also a term for a young (unmarried) lady. Or you could call an older lady xiaojie and win some major points.
10. *Jianghu* literally means rivers and lakes, but it's the catchall term for the martial arts world and its surrounding community. Also known as the underworld, it's a loose culture of itinerant martial artists, merchants, doctors, priests. It's a social space of sorts where people are away from family and find family on the road. There are very few rules, and you can think of it like the Wild West.
11. See the story Neigui in *Tales of the Swordsman Vol. 1*.
12. See The Magistrate's Vow in *Tales of the Swordsman Vol. 2*.
13. See The Runaway's Homecoming in *Tales of the Swordsman Vol. 1*.

Chapter 2

1. He actually doesn't do any of his own cleaning either. . . .
2. Qinggong is also known as 'lightness' Kung Fu. Through the manipulation of qi, people are able to perform acrobatic feats and practically 'fly.'

Chapter 3

1. Baomu is a nanny.
2. The best translation of this is "knight errant" or literally a martial hero. If you've ever encountered a wuxia hero, then you've encountered a *xiake*.
3. Magistrate Tao Jun *may* have roughed him up a few times. Maybe.
4. Martial arts skill.
5. A "high hand" or a master of something. You can be a cooking *gaoshou* or even a video game playing *gaoshou*. It's actually quite a useful term that can be used to describe a level of skill in any interest.
6. Yes, this is an elaborate BTS joke.
7. See *Duel at Broken Furniture Inn*.
8. The erhu is a two-stringed bowed instrument.
9. Those reasons can be found in *Tales of the Swordsman*.
10. (Not actually Li Ming's daughter) see *Fangs of the Black Tiger*.
11. See *Broken Chair, Hidden Fist*.
12. Wait, was he carrying an arrow this whole time? Where was he hiding it? Makes you wonder about how accurate his story is.

Chapter 4

1. A small gazebo-like pavilion that can often be found on the side of the road as a resting area, or a viewing area.
2. Watch out: he will trap you in a corner at a party and talk about how his sword was made for moonlight duels. Sometimes people misunderstand and think he's propositioning them and then are surprised to find out that he really is just talking about his sword.
3. Is it over Anakin?

Chapter 5

1. A bo is a type of cymbal.
2. Tao Jun *may* have threatened to burn down their monastery.
3. Huangjiu or 'yellow' wine is a popular type of wine brewed from rice or millet. There's a whole range of flavor profiles ranging from dry to sweet.

Chapter 6

1. Actually, he doesn't do the paperwork. He just pawns it off on Ji Ping who does it and then Tao Jun stamps his seal and signs his name. Still, it's a lot of stamping to do. And he's got to sit there and wait. Such a hard life.
2. Dantian is also known as the Field of Elixir. It's believed to be where the life force or qi of the body resides.

3. *Jiu* is wine.
4. Martial arts.

Chapter 7

1. Bully. He means bully.
2. One of the principles of ancient Chinese law is that a person could not be convicted without a confession.

    This is great!

    It also meant that magistrates would extract confessions with torture to get that confession—not so great.

Chapter 8

1. By now you should be realizing just how much Tao Jun lies. Can we even trust this story?
2. When dealing with dramatic assassins, it's important to be dramatic.
3. You know, Tao Jun does all these things to avoid paperwork, but I'm pretty sure this kind of a mess creates MORE paperwork.

    Poor Ji Ping.

Chapter 9

1. See *The Peacock* in *Tales of the Swordsman Vol. 1*.

ALSO BY JF LEE

I am building a connected world of wuxia heroes and stories. Here are some highlights!

Enjoy what you read? **Get a free story** when you sign up for my newsletter. This light hearted spoof on martial art tropes is sure to put a smile on your face.

Duel at Broken Furniture Inn

https://dl.bookfunnel.com/5zrxylokh0

Yan Tao's daily routine as the proprietor of the Green Brocade Inn is similar to most other proprietors: manage the books, order ingredients, train the staff, greet guests.

And clean up broken furniture.

Green Brocade is better known by its nickname in the world of the *jianghu* — the Broken Furniture Inn. For some reason, the popular stopping place draws in martial artists intent on proving their honor and settling grudges. Yan Tao is tired of heroes wrecking his place and his inn is always another brawl away from bankruptcy. But when a group of bandits appears, the fate of his inn rests in the hands of a young pugilist with a mysterious past.

ALSO BY JF LEE

THE TALES OF THE SWORDSMAN

Vol. 1

Sword of Sorrow, Blade of Joy

There is only one kind of justice in the jianghu: the kind you bring with a sword.

After maiming a nobleman's son, Shu Yan thought the best place to hide was in the company of a legendary swordsman. But she certainly didn't expect to join him in his quest to find the man who murdered his master and family.

Li Ming is the last swordsman of Blue Mountain. He has sworn an oath to avenge his master's death and bring the man who murdered his family to justice.

But in the search for his master's killer, the swordsman and the runaway girl will face bandits, conmen, conspiracies, and scheming nobles. Because the road to revenge is never straight, and always full of danger.

Inspired by classic Kung Fu films and spaghetti western movies, Sword of Sorrow, Blade of Joy is the first volume of tales of the swordsman—adventures of wuxia action, witty banter, martial arts camaraderie, bandits, princesses, and treacherous villains.

Vol. 2

Fangs of the Black Tiger

Bounty hunters have taken Shu Yan.

To save the girl, Li Ming, the last swordsman of Blue Mountain, must call on the aid of his old allies: the deadly spearwoman Jingyi, and Tao Jun, his sworn brother (and occasionally corrupt magistrate).

Meanwhile, Shu Yan, in the company of the most ruthless and dangerous scum of the martial world, must rely on more than her wits and a snarky joke to survive.

But there is unrest in the martial world. Shazha Kui, the butcher of Blue Mountain, has resurfaced at the head of a powerful army, intent on toppling an empire.

Has the time finally come for Li Ming to avenge the ghosts of his family?

Vol. 3

Fall of the King Saber

Coming soon! Subscribe to my newsletter for more updates on when this is coming out.

LOOKING FOR MORE?

Join the Cultivation Novel Group on Facebook for more recommendations and discussion about Wuxia, Xianxia, and Cultivation novels.

ABOUT THE AUTHOR

JF Lee currently resides in the Cayman Islands. He loves a good hat and telling stories about heroes with swords in wuxia settings. He's always thinking about the next adventure to write and where it'll take him. When he's not working on his next novel, he can be found diving for green sea turtles to photograph.

Stay Updated
For the latest in writing and updates, sign up for JF Lee's newsletter at JFLee.co
or join his Facebook group at https://www.facebook.com/JFLeeAuthor/.

Printed in Great Britain
by Amazon